As If

As If
and other stories

by Alban Goulden

Anvil Press Publishers | Vancouver

Anvil Press Publishers Inc.
P.O. Box 3008, Main Post Office
Vancouver, B.C. V6B 3X5 Canada
www.anvilpress.com

Library and Archives Canada Cataloguing in Publication information is available upon request.

ISBN 978-1-77214-048-4 (paperback)

Printed and bound in Canada
Cover lettering by Sean Welby
Cover design by Rayola Graphic Design
Interior by HeimatHouse
Represented in Canada by the Publishers Group Canada
Distributed by Raincoast Books

The publisher gratefully acknowledges the financial assistance of the Canada Council for the Arts, the Canada Book Fund, and the Province of British Columbia through the B.C. Arts Council and the Book Publishing Tax Credit.

To me, for finally doing it.

And to Brian Kaufman, editor and publisher, without whose recognition of its value, and light but sure touch, this book wouldn't be.

TABLE OF CONTENTS

THE ALL-MEAT EMPRESS CAFÉ

"All Meat. All Kinds. All Good."

Dan says he got the idea in the back of the Medicine Hat Safeway.

Had to take a piss real bad. In answer to his query, the half-balding clerk jerked a finger towards the swinging doors. "In back. Only for customers," he said, but the doors were already swinging.

The can was filled with floor mops and buckets. As Dan sighed, zipped up, and came out, he heard and smelled it first. Then, behind the piled up bottles and boxes of dry goods, he glimpsed a huge enclosure shimmering beyond some kind of force field at the south end of the building. He walked cautiously towards the stink of shit-filled straw and bawling animals. Once beyond the boxes, he could see the killing fields, with only that eye-elusive shimmer between him and all the action. Men and women in filthy full-length rubber coveralls strode with their guns, huge knives, and blacksmith hammers at the ready amongst a chaotic mess of chickens, cows, pigs, goats, lambs, horses, and flopping fish. All screaming. Even the fish, he swears now. Throats cut. Limbs, fins, heads hacked off. Bullet to the brain or sometimes just into the eye. Slam of hammer against skulls. Animals howling fear and terror. Humans cursing them for their stubborn unwillingness to die. Blood spurting in fountains. Carnage as far as Dan could see.

The workers took breaks for gulps of cold beer and ice water, sweat running down to mix with the drying brown-red guts strewn over their coveralls.

"You're not supposed to be here," a thin voice beside him said.

"So this is where the meat comes from," Dan breathed. "Back of Safeway. Really."

"We have lawyers. *Extreme* methods of enforcement," Thin Voice said.

"What?"

"Legal. You can't say anything. Ever. You a meat eater?"

Dan gave him a look.

Thin Voice gestured. "Okay, okay. Pick, then. Has to be a live one. You have to kill it. Feed it to somebody innocent. Kid. Old lady. Someone who thinks meat grows in Safeway in cellophane-wrapped packages. And," he came close so he could whisper, "you have to put a little bit of your blood in the final product. Just a touch. Nothing to cause any problems."

Much later, in the telling of it to me here in the village of Empress, Alberta, Dan gets more and more excited. This Safeway experience is what led him to one of his famous "Big Ideas": an Alberta restaurant that specializes in every kind of meat—and only meat.

"So you did it," I say to him in the Agro Building where he runs *The All-Meat Empress Café*. His establishment shares the place with a combo two-sheet curling and winter skating rink that right now is just prairie dirt. His is the only café remaining in this village that is on the way to hamlet, sinking back into the cacti and rattlesnakes.

"Yeah, yeah. Course. Why not? Soon as I got back from the Hat I had the kids in here. Gave 'em an un-birthday party to celebrate the opening. Lot of the parents came too. Specially the fat mothers. Gorged on burgers."

"And your blood."

"Hell, they never noticed. Mr. Thin Voice said it's a matter of a quick infection. He just wants to get them hooked: y'-know, meat from the back of Safeway."

"Whatever happened to 4-H clubs?" I mutter.

"No one wants a direct interface anymore," he says.

"You like that word 'interface.'"

"Heard it in the Yukon when I was cooking at the camps. Bikers. Drugs. Beatings in the bar. An execution here and there. Well, it was a long way from Whitehorse. Fresh air that would kick-start your ass. Some of those bikers are pretty educated, eh. Business degrees. Mounties came in once a month. We handed out beer and sent them on their way. The odd time a bear chewed some guy into hamburger." He looks at me with that sly partly toothless smile. "I know my new idea's gonna excite you."

Dan is Mexican-Italian-Palestinian. He looks like a soccer player gone to seed—especially after a night of drinking and then attempting to smile through the toothless gaps. He likes to shock me because I'm female. Probably thinks it's a kind of seduction. I imagine his mouth on me and shiver. *Not* in that way.

"I know what you're thinking," he says. "I quit drinking after what happened in Safeway. Had to dedicate myself to the vision."

I've heard his *I'm-not-drinking-anymore* lies too many times already. "I don't care about that," I say. "How'd you get through the force field?"

He shrugs. "Thin Voice. He muttered something into a thing on his wrist and it let me through. Said if he hadn't neutralized it, I would of been skinned alive."

"You believed him."

"I believed all of it. Still do."

"Horseshit," I say.

"A lot of that there, for sure. Anyway. He told me I had to use the blacksmith hammer, so I picked out a young steer—squished a couple of chickens as I moved in."

"You weren't... I don't know... a little upset?"

"I've killed before," he says enigmatically. "Stood me in good stead. Goddamn thing wouldn't die right away. Looked at me with those big, crazy, fuckin' terrified eyes. Mr. Thin Voice told me to get pissed off at them. Makes it easier. But I already knew that from before. From the Yukon."

"So... you beat the crap out of the steer."

"Took a while." He shrugs again. "Way it goes sometimes. A real mess when I finally beat the fucker's brains out. So much blood already that when I pricked my finger to add mine it disappeared into the rest right away."

"Your whole story is madness," I say. "Crazy."

"Where the fuck d'you think your bacon, chicken burgers, and steaks come from, huh? They should take everybody back there and make 'em shoot, stab, hit, slash, and hack. I guarantee they'd value their cutlets more and that's a fact. I always knew those Yukon bikers really appreciated life after a night in the elimination business. Why they took it slowly. There's technique even in death, eh. I learned a lot from them."

I stumble outside into the cold air, take a big gulp of it. Snow slants against my face, stinging.

Across the empty spaces of dead grass now turning white, I see the squat post office and the abandoned United Church that in a distant life was a hotel and bar. Behind me I feel the bulky presence of *The All-Meat Empress Café*. A whiff of sweet meat wafts past me as the door opens.

He joins me. "Nice place here," he says. "Empress. Nobody bothers anybody. They only know as much as they want to and fight against anything more. Ignorance. Bliss. Well, maybe 'bliss' is too strong a word…"

"Who are you to make those kinds of judgements? These are good people."

He doesn't answer. We stand for a while.

Finally: "You never asked me about my new Big Idea. The details." He holds up a bandaged forefinger. Waving it, he sticks out his tongue at me, looks me up and down, and licks the air with it. Laughs at my reaction. "You're cute like that. How come you got no boyfriend?"

"Uh." I don't want to talk to him. He can be so creepy. And I am still thinking about the force field. Only thing that makes sense is aliens.

"What I like about the back of Safeway is they don't waste

anything," he muses. "Blood. Guts. All into the dog food, hamburger, chicken nuggets, whatever. Like the Germans say, 'Everything that's *fleisch*.' Flesh. Meat." He lights a smoke, draws deeply, and spews it into the driving snow—and my face. Smiles at me. "Made a deal with some foreign paramilitaries."

I throw him a look of disgust. And move upwind. I hate cigarette smoke.

AS IF

"The body is as complex as any thought process we can have."
—Édouard Lock

As if it were that easy. A blind roll of the universe dice.

Rye's trashed Adidas (supposed to wear safety boots), bare hands (supposed to wear work gloves), air of salt-fresh Fraser River lifting hair (supposed to wear hard hat). A leap without looking onto a raft of logs, grafter pole nonchalant above the head. Done a thousand times. Today a bonus of taffy sun oozing across sky blue; new towers and old slag buildings of New Westminster gleaming like they belong together.

He never looks down because it's as easy as taking a breath.

Except this once. Neimi calls out as Rye is mid-air between the tug and the raft. He hears every predictable thing Neimi says: "Hey, ballerina! Yer wife let you out tonight?" Half-turns, sees Neimi's scraggly head against the tug and the sunshine on New West, the background hill with its top evergreen chunk of Queen's Park dark spires. And he knows something. It bursts up from a place he had not before realized, a revelation, as his head turns slowly back across the bright river to the raft—a leisurely pan of sky/sun/blue/cedar—then down to the logs beneath his feet and the gap between: water, dark and open. *There. That's where it is.*

The decision made, he alters everything, drops the grafter, lets go, and disappears from the world of light.

As if Maureen should know.

Why. That's what they all ask her—cops, media, relatives, the sometimes-friends, people at work.

At night Maureen sits in a chair in a corner of Krystal's darkened room, listening to her child sleep. Sometimes she creeps close to check on the breathing. They are supposed to keep breathing.

What she wants to explain to everyone is her confusion: how can there be death without a body, so you can check on their breathing? She touches her daughter's cheek, warm, imagines blood flooding through legs, arms, head, up and down, it's like a water pump or computer that you depend on every day, every moment but have no idea how it works in spite of diagrams or doctors. Or some of her relatives, the religious nuts sounding like drug pushers who keep babbling to her about "The Forgiving Holy Spirit" at the party after the funeral, especially when she sees the look on their faces. Why haven't these people disappeared from the world?

The behaviour of most of the rest is more conventional: Johnny Walker, Molsons, and that cloying cloak of weed enfolding the young.

At this party she sits in a chair in the corner. They think it is the grief about Rye. But she has to concentrate all her energy on breathing: imagining him lurching, jerking, gulping water for air, his body so angered at the change. His terror. She experiences it over and over. But she can't drink a bottle of vodka or inhale a joint like the rest of them; that would make tomorrow morning impossible. She might as well go jump into the river with him.

Which she has considered.

But her anger at Rye saves her; her body's anger will not allow the booze or the water in. And of course there's Krystal. *Do I love her enough?* She huddles in the corner where the two walls can protect. *Do I love anyone?* She remembers the quote someone sent to her Facebook page: "A hug from the right person can make just about anything better."

And then there was the grasping feel of Ella, her sister, a few hours ago, before Ella flew back to Ottawa. They'd both cried, Ella gulping like a plump seal, her warm tears running down Maureen's cheek into her dress. Maureen had stiffened, fighting an impulse to laugh. Ella had interpreted this as convulsive grief and so grabbed harder. But an indifference opened within Maureen. As if she were watching a rehearsal for a drama in which she might be asked to act as if she could provide proof. *Proof of what? My acting ability?*

She remembers Ella, nine, and herself, five, when her sister and mother had buried the rabbit. After Maureen's racking sobs ceased, she'd looked out the window into the sky where her mother said Flopsy had gone—maniacal, seeking the cloud she now was. And Ella coming quietly behind her, whispering, "She was still alive, you know. When we buried her. *Still...a...live.*"

It crosses Maureen's mind that she can get up, go to her daughter, and easily stop the life they, in the hospital, told her she'd given (when the drugs began to fade they put the small bundle with the screwed-up face in her arms). It's easy to stop anybody's life. The blood, the skin, the silly brain, everything so fragile. Her leg moves forward to get up; she grabs it. *To do what? Am I mad?*

Shivers. Rye would laugh. He has/had no time for imagination. He's all about action.

As if it were possible.

Not to let go. Ice fear as he drops from certainty into panicked *didn't mean to!* Horror love for the world above—Maureen, Krystal, anyone. Instead now this despairing sink into the vicious dark.

Lungs almost empty, head jerks up to receding square of light. The river carries him beneath, away. Flailing legs, arms, spits out remaining air and becomes insane desire to live, upthrusting until open water between the rafts lets him through.

Somehow into air. Sunlight.

The very next thought he claws up a rocky bank in the painful light. Sees his hands shake as they slick over wet dirt and rocks, but he can't feel the shivers. There is a racking cough in his lungs. Mind sinks away...

And wakes to sound. "Neimi?" His own voice?

There's a scrabbling. He is aware of himself pulled roughly along in the slanting sunlight, hears the laboured breathing of someone whose hard work this is.

His possessor stops. He knows it's a woman even before she gasps: "You're harder to haul than a deadhead."

The world seems broken into crystal facets: hard-edged

clarities. There's a single shard of grass just inches from one eye. He notices a tiny blotch curling the end of it. The blotch moves, some kind of bug waving its feelers towards him. Then his vision lurches forward. "Fuck!" he swears. She laughs. The hard light fades.

Some moments later Rye has a dream. He's seated at a table playing cards. Maureen is dealing, but there's a guy beside her who points his fingers at a card she takes off the top of the deck to give to Rye. The man—his name is The Colonel—raises one eyebrow, and she quickly puts the card on the bottom of the deck and takes another off the top. A haze of other players sit around the table, but Rye knows they're not important.

The guy next to Maureen keeps changing. One moment he's young, dark-haired, a trimmed black beard; then he's elegant, grey-haired, with one wandering eye. Then he looks like the Canadian Forces colonel who turned out to be a serial rapist/killer.

Rye turns up his cards. They're blank. He puts all his chips in anyway—four mil. The Colonel grins at him. "Can't get hurt if you're shootin' blanks," he says, his eyebrow raised.

As if he were there.

The next image is river morning. Mist drifts, curls over the water; a rising sun burns it away. He's sitting on a rickety porch, blanket wrapped around him. Distant groan of waking container cargo machines; a spiritual exhaustion inside. Cup of steaming tea in front of him: wisps of fragrant heat. Like a plant seeking light, he brings it to his lips, feels the hot tang roll into his mouth and down, spreading warmth.

Rye looks up. A woman somehow very familiar, grey streaks in her hair, drops into the chair opposite, takes a deep breath, and gazes at him. Her eyes are full of experience, not hard but absorbing.

Rye becomes nervous, gulps tea, and chokes. She waits him out. When he can breathe normally she says, "It's not easy coming back to life, being born again. Time can slide. I know."

"What?" he croaks.

"I saw you out there," she says, flicking her head towards the river. "You didn't slip. It wasn't an accident. You just let go, dropped into it all on your own."

He puts the tea down on the porch. "I don't know what I did. Or why. I don't feel like I decided anything. It just came to me...happened. Something my body did."

"Huh. Well that's a big thing to do on the spur of the moment." She sighs and reaches over, sticks out her hand. "My name's Maureen."

Rye's head comes up; he jerks back into the chair, holds the blanket tight around him. "Oh, God," he says.

"I admit it's not the greatest name," she half laughs, misunderstanding. "And I'm not even Irish. My Ukrainian parents thought Maureen was English. Desperate to blend in, eh."

Rye looks up at the sky to turn his attention another way. "Why am I here?"

Maureen does laugh. "Hah! You'll have to figure that out for yourself, boyo. I've got work to do. No time for epistemology."

"Huh?" Rye says.

As if he *never* existed.

The thought is surprising to Maureen. She tastes its strangeness. Grief at Rye's death has become a black gulf between now and her past. A gulf that's growing. She can see this receding landscape break into coruscating light that fades into rerun convention: the night after their wedding when he had tears in his eyes; the Thanksgiving Day Maureen's father got drunk and cracked one of Rye's ribs and how Rye manoeuvred his way through the cops just for her; the way he often sat with Krystal on his lap as they both stared at the hockey game on TV. (Krystal checking on Rye's open face that is like the face of a child too…Krystal making sure she was doing the right thing, copying her dad's cheering, swearing.)

And other memories: the way he would become a wild madman during sex exactly when Maureen wanted him to; the way she caught Rye and her sister, a then still-thin Ella, looking at each other when they didn't know her understanding had knifed through—of course, they didn't know she'd seen the email, airhead Ella babbling: "*My feelings—temporarily crushed because I am not seen as realistic but a fantasist. Rye, you and I have greater communication of mind and soul than I ever experienced with anyone before, male or female…magnetism that creates stronger energies to deal with people. Maybe, Rye, that is not allowing you a true self of what you feel…but I want to make me a stronger person, self-reliant and God-loving in the energies that soar from our creativity of spirit…*"

Now all of it—especially Ella's babbling—belongs to someone else in some other place. There is a clean, clear emotional space around her, a kind of open field. It's as if her body knows she can turn in any direction, go any way. It's not that the other person—that other Maureen who used to be her—doesn't still want him, miss him, not that the memories don't make love and sentiment wash around her, but he is not at the centre of the new Maureen.

She's not sure what should be there.

As if he dreams he died in the river.

Fierce currents pushing him down into darkness, bubbles trailing, the complete dread of knowing his body will make him die. But first fighting it. Alone. Grey-dark. Abandoned. Everything out of his control. "Mommy help me!" he opens his mouth. Sharp pain like a blow to his chest. Then a terrifying cold warmth, terrifying because he knows it is the beginning of death. A cool light at the bottom of the river moving towards him, implacable.

"Hey!" a voice says, "McKinn. You'll burn out your eyes facing the sun like that."

He shudders awake. Sergeant Cameron is a haloed shadow above him.

"Sorry, Sarge." He sits up, spitting dust. The squad is at the side of the road, Highway 1, right in the middle of "Ambush Alley." To the south he can see the distant yellow-brown gleam of the Registan. *Country of sand, all right*, he thinks, remembering the dust-billowing convoys. North, Kandahar is about an hour away.

Sergeant Cameron ambles back to the armoured carrier.

Bastion says in his ear, "That prick gonna hit a Terminator some time now."

"Cameron's okay," he says. "Only reason you don't like him is because *you're* such an asshole."

"Me! 'E 'ave it for me, you can be sure 'bout dat, Pete."

He looks away into the dry, yellow-grey distance of the land rising towards the north and east. Somewhere beyond Afghanistan are the Himalayas. Cool snow. Lakes. Water rippling over rivers of stone. Fantasies of the Rockies.

"Bastion, I don't like you calling them Terminators. They're just fucking roadside bombs, eh."

"Hah, Pete. I ask you again when you step on 'im."

"Ya, ya." He pushes himself up through the hot air, bends to pick up his rifle, then twists swiftly towards Bastion. "What did you call me?"

Bastion laughs. "I call you lot of tings, eh."

"No, not that. You called me 'Pete.'"

Bastion gives him a strange look. "*Oui*, I call you Pete. *C'est vrai.*"

"Why? That's my brother, he's in—" *My brother Pete is in Afghanistan.*

Just before they get underway, Sergeant Cameron passes on an order from Lieutenant Goodrow to send them ahead on point to check for the telltale signs of roadside mines: odd-looking rises or depressions, especially for anything hastily covered with dirt, grass, or brush.

Walking at the highway's edge, he remembers the rattlesnake at his uncle's on the prairie. It's a hot day like this, but in the late afternoon the young snake is out sunning on the gravel road, blended. Rye jogs in a far zone, fantasizing. As he takes another step, he sees the snake in his peripheral vision and angles his leg aside on the way down, watches his foot descend, an action beyond conscious decision, watches it come down on the slight depression in the road. Of course, then it is too late for Pete.

As if Maureen recognizes the wolf at her door.

She bites her lip, watching him sit in the sun and stare at the river. He looks innocuous, vulnerable. *But that's always the case, isn't it? The vulnerable ones are the most dangerous. Like a snake invisible in the road. The world lulls you into thinking it's a safe place until your lover, your child, your corporate government, the voice in the whirlwind demands: 'What do you know? What can you do if we take it all away?'*

Thankfully, he's a stranger now. Yet there's something familiar about him, as if her body remembers why. Something that locks into a place inside, a heartbreaking place where she is young and susceptible, long before the stone in the graveyard—now she wonders whose is it, really? A time, like now, when Rye abruptly appears and seems the answer to every question about her future but god help her not her past.

She shakes her grey-streaked hair; glad the child is at her mother's, not here. What will she do with this bizarre coincidence that can't possibly be, this new yet strangely familiar man? A man who would throw his life away to get it back. As she did.

LIE TO ME OR I'LL PANIC

There's rain falling from the Vancouver sky and nothing will make it go away. We're on the campus of Language College. Through the downpour I can see, far above me, part of the shimmering orange "Lang—" sign near the top of the main building.

"Let's get inside before we drown," Marie growls, "or someone steps off that roof."

She's black as African night, so I can hardly see her in the murk. I agree. No way I want a body landing on me: disappointed students and instructors are a problem in these places.

We fight our way to the entrance against the hordes attempting to break out into illusory freedom. They're babbling on their phones—and not in English. I hear Mandarin,

Korean, Russian, Tagalog, Punjabi, Italian...the cultural con-querors of the Lower Mainland burst through the doors like a bunch of lemmings on their way to a cliff party.

Once we make it inside, the crowds melt away and it's rel-atively quiet. We shake the water off and Marie smiles, blinding white teeth emerging out of black. Her smile can make me do almost anything. "You stay down here," she says. "I'll head up. Use your cell if you discover something."

I nod. One of the main difficulties in these missions is the lack of a complete context, but they all begin so suddenly we never have time to check with the Ministry. Not that it would help. The Ministry usually knows even less than we do, their main job being to create what's released to the public.

Sickening squish-thud sounds filter through the doors be-hind us. We turn, there is the thrill of screams, the crowd parts. Near the door I can see corporate trucks with their neon logos. Uniformed staff are picking up the successful re-cruits and loading them into the back of the vehicles.

"It's started," Marie says. "Let's get moving."

"Right," I reply. I'm scared. Nothing can train you for the times when all signs indicate rationality has gone sideways. And what better place for it than a college campus where the belief in reasoned order is as powerful as in Parliament. But when you're promised a Rapture and sell your house only to find transcendence has been postponed until next year—or the Canucks don't win the Stanley Cup. Again...

When manic denial and subterfuge fail, people go bananas.

As usual, the Ministry doesn't expect us to do anything about it. Just observe and document. Why? How can a litany of failures help a determinedly ignorant species gain self-knowledge? Marie claims it's a matter of transference and projection. But then who am I to understand failure—or success, for that matter.

I watch her head for the stairs, and I remember my mother.

She's inert in the bed. Her doctor has already given the pep talk of what a great life she's had, what wonderful children she's produced. Message: game over. Then the doctor leaves. She looks at me—a strange curiosity in her eyes. She knows she has encouraged me to lie to her all my life, lie to her as a form of love. Of loyalty. Her eyes say, "Lie to me one more time. Prove to me you love me even if you don't. Lie to me or I'll panic. And you won't be able to handle that."

I'm afraid I can't do it. Then I'm afraid I can. I'm afraid of what she'll do. So I gamble and tell the truth. She panics. Then vomits, chokes on it. I run, yelling for a nurse. I look back and see that her eyes are amused even as her body flails, inhaling the puke.

Now I shake my head. Waste of time thinking of it.

I stay on the main Language College floor and walk down a hall that has stairs branching downwards to basement-level lecture rooms. There's a door at the bottom of the stairs and it's open. Somebody's pontificating. I carefully tiptoe to the entrance, pull back against the open door, and peek in. A guy stands at the front, punctuating his thin-voiced points with the Don Cherry thumbs up. He's in his early thirties, dressed in a business suit sans jacket, shirtsleeves rolled two turns neatly back so a roiling dragon tattoo just shows at the top of his left wrist. His sixties' retro tie is askew. He was skinny a couple years ago, but the beer and weed are beginning to plump him up. He's talking about Vancouver's latest hockey riot.

"Everyone thinks," he says slowly, "that this was a one-off.

Beautiful Vancouver's fall from Olympic grace. How could it happen? Well, the news is Vancouver's always had riots. The first suicide, uh, I mean riot—" he pauses meaningfully. "You hear what I just said? A Freudian slip, eh. Which means? Anyone?" He waits for a response.

I peek further around the corner. There's a homogenous sea of young faces—South Asian, East Asian, Japanese, African, Iranian, German, Russian, including a few Caucasian—staring in noncommittal indifference at him.

"Freud? Yes? No?"

Finally a thin, light-haired blond raises her hand.

"Irina." He points to her, but no one else turns to look.

"Means accident thinking. Think one word but say other one reveals subconscious meaning. Is reference to Jewish psychoanalysis."

"Uh…yeah," he responds. "Freud was actually Austrian. And, yes, he was Jewish, a psychoana-*lyst* from the beginning of the twentieth century. Close enough." He pauses a moment, then says, "Say, Irina. I've always wondered where you're from."

Irina squirms, turns red. "Irkutsk," she says quietly.

He smiles. "Russia. You must like hockey, eh? How'd you know about Freud?"

Again Irina squirms. "In high school study Dostoevsky."

"Ah. The great Russian writer. I'd like to talk to you about him sometime."

He does not see the miniscule shake of her head as he resumes. "Now. Vancouver riots. Most authorities agree on eleven in total, but that number is not written in stone. Here's a list of the major ones."

He turns to the overhead and begins to write, reading out

loud as the ink squiggles across the projection: "1887 race riot ...1907 race riot...1938 homeless and unemployed riot...1963 and 1966 Grey Cup riots...1971 Hippy Gastown riot...1994 hockey riot..."

Somebody throws a bottle. It bounces off the blackboard, and the professor turns in surprise, yelling, "Hey—!" And is hit in the face by a heavy textbook. Blood spurts out of his nose. Another bottle catches him in the head and he goes down like a rock, sprayed red running over the now messed-up list of riots on the overhead. A chorus of enthusiastic howls bursts forth and bottles begin flying everywhere. Shocked, I pull back. My days as a student were never like this.

My cell rings. I flip it open and hear Marie yelling: "You gotta get up here!"

"No," I answer. "You need to see what *I'm l*ooking at!" I'm about to cam and show her but she growls, "Just get your ass up here. Now! Third floor, west side."

"But—okay. Be right there." She's my boss and my goddess, eh.

I sneak back up the stairs away from the sounds of the melee. Someone has closed the door, but I still hear sickening thumps against the wall and cries of terror and pain punctuated by every racist curse possible.

It occurs to me that while I'm on this job I'm in a dream world. Events happen that lurch towards meaning but jump from image to metaphor rather than following any kind of linear chronology. Is that what narrative really is? A combination of incomplete external similes and mushy subjectivity?

Truth is I'm afraid of what I imagine, what I might see next. I'm addicted to pornography, for example, but I keep lying about it to everyone else, especially Marie. Guilt. Guilt.

So on the next floor I make myself look straight ahead and not into the classrooms where I know horny young women are making out. Asses in the air. Big, thick cocks waiting their turn. I take the stairwell two steps at a time. And this fear makes me a terrible lover. Women know I'm afraid to look at them, that I leap away instead.

But self-loathing is a pleasure I'd hate to give up.

When I finally find Marie after running a rat's maze of corridors on the third floor, she's pointing to a stairway leading to the roof. There's a lineup of students at the bottom of it. They are desultorily texting and talking, their awkward backpacks swinging behind them as they slowly climb. We excuse ourselves as we push through the lineup.

"What's happening?" I ask the students. "What's going on up there?"

Most don't even bother to look at me, or they screw up their faces as if I'm speaking English or another foreign language.

I look at Marie but she shrugs.

Oh. One other thing: some of the students are crying softly, mascara running on the girls' faces, the boys quietly sobbing. When I was in grade five in Connaught Elementary School in Medicine Hat, we used to have lineups like this for the strap every morning. We had a substitute teacher from England. He was short and wore a Chaplin moustache. He had the idea that English public school techniques could be used to create "young men and women of character." Eventually some official informed him that strapping in schools was illegal now, even in Alberta.

By the time we elbow our way to the roof, I can see what looks like an instructor off to the side of the line that is slowly moving towards the edge of the building. I can hear the corporate trucks with their engines running in front of the entrance below.

"Shit," Marie says. "It's exactly what I thought it would be."

As we approach her, the instructor looks up from the notes she is taking, gives us an inquiring smile.

"Help you?" she says. "Can't talk long. Middle of an exam."

We both flash our Ministry I.D.s.

"Oh," she says, "you're here to observe. Fine then."

Marie nudges me.

"Well," I say. "We do have a question."

"Cool," she says, intent on making plus and minus signs in her notes. I should also mention that she is hardly much older than her students. I catch her giving a conspiratorial smile to a few crying favourites as they shuffle to the front of the line.

Marie can't wait for me and spits at her, "What class is this exactly?"

The teacher raises an eyebrow. "Oh. Didn't they tell you? Psych class. This is the final exam." She consults her watch, turns to the students, and yells, "Stop!"

The line shuffles to a halt. Heads swivel towards her.

"Pee break for those who want it. Back in five."

Nobody moves.

She pivots towards us on her fake, calfskin urban guerrilla boots. Her voice tips up interrogatively at the end of every sentence. "I sense, y'know, a dissing tone in your voice. Like, you disapprove?"

Marie shrugs. "Just doesn't seem too efficient."

"The philosophy of this class is...wait a minute—" she rifles through papers— "ah, here: *To provide the student with practical experience in self-destructive masochism as a major pedagog-*

31

ical activity that edges the line between pleasure and pain, risk and reward. Students will be expected to grasp how conditioning of the individual is the essence of successful participation in the social sphere. This course may not be repeated.'"

She sorts the papers back into place. "Actually," she says, "we're an interdisciplinary crossover course that also engages modes from both sociology and anthropology."

"You mean these are the kinds of things you make these poor, pathetic little shits go through in order to get an 'A'?" I say, suddenly angry.

"Everyone sacrifices a part of themselves to join society," she answers. "It's a trade-off."

"But the deck is stacked! Success is the worst thing that can happen to them!"

"Ah," she says. "You have grasped the essential contradiction. Every society sacrifices its youth to blind self-destructive behaviours, idiotic wars, or mindless consumption. It enforces the social swarm. Anyway, most kids are brain-empty. You ever look at their texting? *'Ya, like…ohmygod!'*" She parrots. "And it's easy to make more of them. Older people, like me—or you, for that matter—have expensive social knowledge. We're keepers. Besides, we've already voluntarily abandoned the core of our identity selves."

"So what's *our* reward?"

She smirks. "Oh, we're each allowed a secret addiction or two that keeps us hooked." She looks straight at me. "Betcha I know yours!"

I take a step back, feel a sick lump in my stomach.

"Ever have problems getting people into this class—or with attendance?" Marie asks.

The instructor arches her eyebrow again. "This course is

always full at the beginning of each semester. Attendance is excellent. Well…at least until the exam," she says. But then she swivels back to her students. "Okay! Break's over. Keep moving! No pissing your pants now guys!" She laughs.

I reach towards the instructor. I'm surprised to note that there's a fist at the end of my arm.

Marie grabs it. "You can't!" she hisses. "No matter what you think. We observe. Make notes. You know the drill."

"Damn this job," I say.

"Just put it in your report," she says. "That's where it belongs. Stop feeling sorry for yourself and let others worry about it." She begins to make notations on her phone. Then turns to me.

"Oh, yeah. I know about the porn too." She smiles a beautiful black and white. "Do us both a favour and stop lying to me. I can handle it."

VAMPYR AT THE MOVIES

You start out on a wide road full of so many possibilities. But each choice you make, I mean, it kind of narrows as you move along, it takes a certain direction. And then you try to bring in other things, good ideas, but well, now they just can't live in that world.

—David Lynch (sort of)

I'm walking across a bridge. It rises in a long curve into the night beyond me, and I can't see the other side where it descends. The peak, at first almost level with my head, drops gradually as I walk towards the moon that sits like a half-starved albino above it. To the moon's right, a comet arrow is aimed at the horizon.

I defy it; I defy them all. But Calpurnia shakes her head and says, *Alas! my lord. Your wisdom is consum'd in confidence.*

Quiet! I hiss at her, annoyed and depressed. It's disheartening to discover that the partner you live with is the part of yourself that demoralizes you. I have no more ideas on how to run away from that.

Calpurnia fumbles at me, always wanting attention. She knows I never really listen to her. On the other hand, every time she predicts a disaster it comes true. But who needs that?

In a fit of predictable masochism I shove her away. The wind pushes the smell of my love's perfume back to me as she slips off the edge of the walkway, falling onto the road. A Number 17 bus hits her straight on. There is a heavy thud in my stomach.

But I cannot cry; instead lurch away, stumble on.

All this happens before.

She keeps warning me, and I keep killing her.

One of my ancient mentors, long consigned to the archives, tells me, *I believe that if you're not fulfilled, you can't create; you can only deconstruct what could have been—that's tragedy.*

The water is a familiar velvet black slopping against the boats anchored beneath the bridge. Pungent smells of blood-rare, charbroiled flesh dusted in Montreal steak seasoning drift up from one of the restaurants on the island beneath the bridge. It makes my stomach growl until I realize I don't deserve even the dead after what I keep doing to Calpurnia.

I try to be happy because I have a desperate need to create, to be loved. For example, the clean breeze off the bay is tinged by traces of diesel oil and garbage, so I will that away in order to make the world a better place. Environmentalism starts in the mind, eh.

By the time I reach the crest of the bridge, I've almost convinced myself.

More of the glittering city spreads like cold diamonds beneath the sinking comet.

Approaching me is an indistinct figure. As he nears, I hear his laboured breathing and see one side of his face twisted in a rictusl smile like some ancient mortal who's had a stroke. This is the guy who I dream tries to push me over the railing into the dark-water night or onto the road.

One more time I can only hope, even as I know it won't work. It never does. As he passes, I will psychic energy at him: *Do it! Do it!* But he turns his warped face away. I can see the poor man is desperately content, that he cannot take on the burden of ending my desire. After all, he's not the one condemned.

If I could, I would do it myself. But it would be useless: there is no bus for me. Not for the first time do I resent Calpurnia and her tricks. A cloaked leap into the velvet ink far below might be a welcome distraction, but then I can't deal with imagining my death, so it would be pointless. Cowards want someone else to live it, I guess.

Now that I'm here, I know hell is the awareness of being trapped in meaningless repetition.

I remember what we are doing back there—before I find myself on this bridge—all of us sitting in the darkened room and staring at the flickering square of light, watching her, the vulnerable stranger.

She looks at us, piteous, even repulsive in her pathetic

hopelessness. Can't she see that even the blood she will not feed on can be made in a factory? Tears line her face but she seems unaware of them. Then I see it—*she* pities *us*! I want to howl at her that it is her world that has collapsed around her. She is the one kneeling in the street amidst the ruins of her house and family, a dead child in her numbed arms—around her a television broken into a million pieces and a deluded civilization feeding off itself.

I've seen all of this before in a movie, but I can't remember its name.

I see the way the white light haloes her. Something inside of me, some distant memory, a desire to comfort, brings her tears into my eyes, and I rise from my seat and move towards the woman. As my hand reaches out and we almost touch, I feel the increasing panic of the others around me. Several hands—frantic—grab my arms; I am shoved roughly back into my seat.

She stares into my eyes, then beyond me.

I can see that she is already dead, and the moment to help has passed. All I can do is feed on her image, my choices long over; feed like the rest of them as they crouch and growl in the terrible darkness around me, their minds sucking and tearing at her pale cinematic flesh.

JOY

When Lena and Wayne first got together, they exchanged résumés. Lena insisted on it. "I'm not going to hook up with another guy unless I know what to prepare for. I want major diseases. Past relationship failures. Spiritual attitudes. Pets. School. Jobs. Weird things. All of it. But it's okay if it's not in complete sentences."

Wayne wrote her a long, rambling response. He went into detail about how he had scored the winning goal in a hockey game that went into two overtimes at the Two Nations Rink. *Got a pass across centre, broke in, made a spin move on the defence. Buried it five-hole.* Then he added, *Have to admit on that spin move, most of the time trying it I'd fall flat on my ass.*

He finished with, *Always been the one dumped in a relationship. Never known Jesus Christ or anyone else as my personal saviour. Had a dog once that ran away and joined a wolf pack. Was so good at pretending I liked school that now I'm in university. Was prepared for life by McDonald's. Am a virgin but I've indulged extensively in onanism.*

At the interview, Lena said, "Don't you ever start sentences with a subject?"

"Option was that we didn't need to use complete sentences."

"Okay," Lena said. "Point taken. I like a guy who reads the fine print. And we can work on the rest. But if you've still got hockey ambitions, forget it. I hate those guys you see in the interviews who take their front teeth out during a game."

"No worries there," Wayne replied. "My big moment was that goal. It was my MVP and Stanley Cup rolled into one. I quit the next day even though the coach said he wouldn't date my sister no more."

Lena fixed him with a straight stare. "I want you to know, Wayne, that grammar is like real important to me."

"Is really important," Wayne said.

They both laughed, and Wayne kissed her a few moments later.

One night they were sitting in bed after sex, sipping Cokes.

"Y'know," Wayne said, "I was thinking after I failed that exam today that you've got a lot of baggage I should've researched more deeply."

"When you say 'failed' you mean you got ninety-five per cent instead of a hundred."

"It's all relative."

Lena sat up. "What 'baggage'?"

Wayne looked at her. "Well. All that stuff about when your parents were missionaries in Somalia, when you were a kid. The starving people you were imprisoned with, the time they tried to...you know...hurt you. Cut you. Down there."

"Enough. Got it." She took a deep breath. "Are you saying

"...d'you mean that I'm not any good at..." She looked hard at Wayne.

"No, no," he said. "You're wonderful. I didn't mean that at all. I don't know what I meant. I don't know why I said it. That was a long time ago."

"What about you being Cree?" she said.

"What's wrong with that? Because I grew up on a reserve?" He sat up.

"Well... I'm sure that wasn't *Dancing with the Stars*."

Wayne put his arm around her. "I had a pretty good childhood. It's relative. We all get damaged here and there."

He was thinking of when he was six and the time his father was drunk and so angry at something that he took Wayne out into the bush and left him there. It was twenty-five below. It got dark. He cried, stumbling around in the snow and bumping into birch and spruce trees until it got too cold and he lay down to sleep. He heard wolves howling and then they were around him. Their eyes gleamed yellow in the dark. He was so terrified he couldn't get air into his lungs. Sling, his dog that had run away to join the pack, came up to him while he was gasping. She licked his face then whined for him to follow her. She led him back to where he could see the cabin. The pack of wolves followed. Sling backed away to join a snarling male as soon as she saw Wayne head for the cabin door. Inside, his father was passed out and his mother had more blood on her face, but she still made him hot soup.

One morning after they'd had a fight and Lena had stomped off in silence to her classes, Wayne took the LRT downtown and walked up 97th. It was becoming more upscale, but in the alleys and in the park to the east there were still people sleeping it off.

41

It comforted him, in a perverse way, like being with some of his relatives again. Something known. He stopped once or twice and tried to cover several unconscious bodies with more cardboard. The sky was a hard grey and he could feel snow coming.

Then he thought how stupid that was and walked back to Jasper Avenue. As he was standing at the intersection, unsure of where to go next, he saw at the opposite corner a couple laughing, arm in arm. The woman leaned into the man's arm as the light changed and they began to cross, deep in animated conversation.

Wayne pulled his collar up and bent his head as he crossed Jasper towards them. They didn't see him.

Lena looked intensely alive, like she was being stimulated on some deep level. Her body seemed magnetically attracted to her psychology professor, his collar-length pepper hair dishevelled just enough to make him look younger and dangerous.

Wayne stumbled. It felt like someone had loosened the connections in his legs. When he reached the opposite sidewalk and turned around, he could see them going into an Italian restaurant. She held the door for her professor, gave him an elaborate bow as he entered, and then followed him in.

Wayne went into a bar and ordered two large glasses of beer. He looked at them for a long time, until the foam had almost disappeared. The waitress came back to him after a while and said, "You want something else? You don't like beer?"

"Yeah, I like it," he said, getting up and throwing another ten on the table. "But I'm afraid of it. Thanks anyway." And he left.

After the punishment of walking home across the Low Level Bridge and almost freezing his feet and his fingers, he made himself watch the unremitting disasters on the news for an hour. Civilians burning. Buildings bombed and burning. Soldiers burning. Politicians who could look serious and plaster on a smile at the same time. People dying of the latest plague in overcrowded intensive care units. A view of the blasted, lifeless moonscape of the Alberta oil sands. Middle-aged men who looked like they'd been sent to the store for a litre of milk but instead had bilked old people out of their life savings. A young man who had taken an axe to six of his high school buddies. A nervous young woman who'd drowned her newborn baby in the toilet.

Then he put on the DVD of the ballet *La Bayadère*. For some reason, ballet made him cry. It was a bizarre world of hopeless beauty: the dancers performing impossible plots and dancing impossible moves, drenched in powerful music that drowned his soul.

When Lena came home, she stood in the doorway for a minute and said, "Sorry about this morning."

"That's okay. I'm sorry too."

She dropped her purse on the floor, flopping onto the couch. "I'm so damned tired."

"Hard day?"

"Yeah."

Then she noticed the Kleenex box and the TV. "What's the matter? Oh. You've been watching ballet again."

"Yeah."

"Anything wrong?"

"Nothing."

A couple weeks later, Lena's father died. The news came in an email from her brother, Dmitri.

"Your brother could of at least phoned us," Wayne said.

"Could *have*. Could *have* phoned us. And that would mean he'd *have* to talk to me." Lena sighed. "He doesn't like talking to me."

"Why?"

"I can be a bitch. Haven't you figured that out yet?"

"C'mon, Lena. You must be feeling pretty bad. Let's go to bed, cuddle, make love."

"Oh, Wayne. You do have a way of saying the right things."

"I love you, Lena. That's all."

After, they lay on their bed, staring up at the dead, white ceiling. Lena said, "Do you know what my dad did? In Somalia?"

Wayne shrugged.

"He converted to Islam after we were captured and separated from each other."

"Huh. Did he do it to try to save you? Were they threatening to chop off everyone's heads? That's how they get conversions sometimes."

"No. Nothing like that."

For a long time Lena was silent. Finally Wayne said, "Well?"

"They told him that if he converted he would go free while they kept the rest of us to ... play with."

"That sounds a bit strange. How do you know this?"

She sighed, raised herself up, and looked at him. "Well, we always wondered why he got released right away and we didn't—at least not until our government finally got off its fat ass. He told me about it when he got really sick once and thought he was dying. He'd made a deal with God that he would tell the truth. So he said he had to tell me."

44

"Did he ever tell your mother, the rest of your family?"

"I don't know. Dmitri thinks I wasn't nice to him just because I'm a bitch." She paused. "He asked me to tell him about the…what they tried to do to me. What it was like."

"Your *brother* asked you that!?"

"No, no." Lena shook her head. "My father. He wanted all the details."

"Why?"

"Huh. I'll leave you to imagine that."

"What did you tell him?"

"That I couldn't remember any of it until I woke up, partly damaged and bandaged in the American hospital."

"Was that true, that you can't remember?"

She turned and whispered in his ear, "What do you think, Wayne? What do you think?"

Two weeks later they were with some friends at a barbecue at Pigeon Lake, south of Edmonton.

"I think you guys are just the cutest couple," Shirley giggled. She took a healthy swallow of her hard lemonade.

The mosquitoes had finally left once the barbecue got really smoking. Pigeon Lake was mostly calm, light ripples tickling its surface in random spots where the breeze touched down.

Azziz nodded. "You got that right. What's your secret? You must be swingers, eh?"

The rest laughed. Weng waved his arms. "It's a kind of weird orthodoxy, y'know. I read somewhere that the highest percentage of swingers are from, like, the American Midwest, that they're mostly Christian fundamentalists. Or at least the children of."

Shirley smiled. "Well *I* think Wayne and Lena truly love each other. They're the opposite of those old Woody Allen movies where everyone worships pain but won't admit it. You know, Allen never really understood Bergman."

"Not the time for your cinema talk, Angie," Azziz said.

"You always call me that. My name's Shirley. Call me by my name."

"A rose by any other ..."

"Oh, just burn it." She gulped down some more lemonade and became very serious. "I think it's because they really know who they are. When you know who you truly are, deep inside, you're ready to accept someone else who knows who they truly are, deep inside. It's the journey of life. It's all good."

"Wow," Weng said. "I hope somebody's taking notes."

Lena had long ago left this conversation and soon found herself alone by the lake. She walked out onto the dock below the summer cabin and the far sounds of the others. A flock of pelicans settled like white knights onto the calm water. They shook their beaks and carried on a dignified, silent debate.

Bugs began to annoy her, but then a sustained breeze came and blew them away. The sun angled against Pigeon Lake, making the brown, shallow water look almost dark blue. In the far distance, someone was water-skiing. She watched as the skier's tips caught the water. The skier flipped end over end—the towline flying—and splattered headfirst into the lake. All this took place in an eerie silence until the motor-boat sound reached Lena. Seconds later, she thought maybe she heard the skier's faint scream. It sounded like someone annoyed, angry.

Then there was just the breeze and the lapping of water against the dock.

For a strange moment, everything seemed to make sense. She looked up at the sky. It was difficult to imagine a hard vacuum on the other side of that blue. *But we have to remember it's there,* she thought. *It's not all good.*

She wondered when she should tell him.

Several days later they were home playing Scrabble. Wayne lost. Lena had managed to make the word "interregnum" by stringing six letters onto "inter."

"I give up," he said.

"Sometimes you give up too easily."

Wayne gave her a mysterious smile. "Sometimes," he said. "But sometimes I also make strategic withdrawals. When there's no king, you have to look out for yourself."

"Hah! Spoken like a future lawyer for sure."

"We hope."

Lena knew it was the time. "I'm pregnant."

Wayne just looked at her.

Was he in shock? She couldn't read his face. She felt the approaching hard edge of panic. "Now we have to make a real commitment," she said. "For the future." Tears appeared in her eyes.

But Wayne at first felt nothing.

Then he thought about his dog that had run away to become a wolf. He imagined Sling standing in front of him, licking, then leading him, the wolf pack at her back. As he turned towards the uncertain cabin door, inexplicably, from somewhere out of the dark forest, came a surge of the purest joy.

'LIKE' IF YOU GET IT

Zuzi starts it off by posting: *Don't believe everything u think.*

Predictably, Zuzi's young gay friend Jbieberlvr tweets: *want his kpcakes.*

Even more predictably from her mother because she thinks it's "cool": *happy happy happy*!!!

Zuzi winces.

A better one from a cousin in Pennsylvania appears on her Facebook page:

"Blonde has a rope around her waist.

Brunette: What are you doing?

Blonde: Trying to kill myself.

Brunette: You're supposed to put the rope around your neck.

Blonde: I tried that but I couldn't breathe.

'LIKE' IF YOU GET IT!"

Andrew's "Today's Headlines" are also interesting:

—*Cute baby competition turns ugly*
—*Man's sex obsession cost his life and is taxable court rules*
—*Visitor drowns on local beach*
—*Man named Nobody misplaced after being rushed to hospital*
—*Mother charged after oven with son's body left on*
—*Body found in airport toilet without luggage*

Almost every day she throws enigmatic statements up on Twitter where they're copied to her Facebook page, and she waits for the responses. Other than being posted on her wall, the winners' replies receive no prize other than a second of star-blip across the cyber universe.

But all of this is really an escape. She has started to spiral into a depression again. It's impossible to get the boy soldier out of her head.

The scene doesn't run like it did on the Internet. Instead, she's there, standing to the side looking up, the crowd claustrophobic, screaming, the boy screaming, gulping, tears running down his face, his eyes animal wild as he twists, hands tied behind his back, legs kicking, the noose pushed over his head and tightened around his neck, the sweat, the men in uniform, the woman beside her piercing her left ear with curses, the boy about ten years old howling out something, maybe "help me, mommy!" or "I kill you!" in some language, the uniformed arms letting him down gently so he can kick and swing and convulse for endless minutes, shit and piss running out of the legs of his pants, convulsive crush of the people next to her, choking, she can't breathe, falling, vomit in her throat and the rest of them trampling her...

Reliving it hardwires it even more deeply. The depression

so overwhelming she can't move: it's like being bound tight in an airless black hole.

But she knows the signs, knows the only way is to make it distant: a memory of a memory.

Then there's Gordo. She has never met him in person. His FB avatar is the smirk face of Charlie Sheen. His "About Me"— "*27, born in Swan River, MB, enthopoesis carjacker & judao-macropathologist*"—isn't much help. If the age listed is correct, he's three years younger than her.

What would Marcus say? She has agreed not to hide from herself or her husband. She knows he can see her doubts. But can he see her hypocrisy? "Facebook is cited as a contributing factor in twenty percent of American divorces" she has read somewhere.

Gordo isn't good for her but she can't dump him. He posts things from the Web that increase her adrenalin levels. And she wants the excitement; it counters the meditation that is supposed to "help" by making her an old-school zombie from the era of her father's leg-dragging *Night of the Living Dead*. She prefers the *28 Days Later* flesh chompers who move like bath salts junkies.

Gordo's specialty is disasters. He posts one every day. Maybe that's why she's interested—he's looking for signs too. Today's link is particularly appealing: *Chris Hedges: This Time We're Taking the Whole Planet With Us* — Truthdig.com: "We seem condemned as a species to drive ourselves and our societies toward extinction, although this moment appears to be the denouement to the whole sad show of settled, civilized life that began some 5,000 years ago."

Gordo's comment beneath the link: *Rapture time*!

Yesterday he posted: "The Earth's Magnetic Field is Failing! You Can Run But You Can't Hide!" He followed it with a jumble of fragments: "...field lost 15% in last 150 years...more cosmic rays, solar radiation...Doomsday taxes overdue...."

The litany of it. All this in her face, in her head—she's drawn to it like the already dead moth. Violence, greed, pain: the most excessive suffering. If an artist invented it, he or she would be accused of impossible hyperbole. Imagining it is like closing her fist over a nail, forcing it millimetre by millimetre into the blood bubbling up around it. *Masochism is to keep me awake,* she writes. *Meditation to dampen the pain.* Now that she's thirty, she believes it's time for her to acquire a sardonic intellectualism. But easier said...

Nothing is more extreme than reality, Zuzi writes on her blog.

On and off she has considered suicide. Her friend Mol says, "I *know* you. Like, you're not *serious.*"

They are sitting in a coffee shop in Yaletown where each cup costs triple what it does at McDonald's (which has better coffee, in Zuzi's view). But Mol likes it here. She calls herself a "performance person—*a PP!*" Giggling. Today she comes dressed in her old Little Flower Academy school uniform. Zuzi sees that the short skirt is unable to cover her thick thighs, nor half-open blouse her bulging boobs. She carries the jacket with her because it can no longer encompass her swollen shoulders. It sits forlornly on the nearest chair.

Zuzi looks at Mol and shudders. It is a question of aesthetics. The only people slobbering over Mol are late middle-aged men who have wads of hair growing out of their ears.

"I know you've got your *problem,*" Mol says quietly, leaning her unevenly chopped purple-pink today's colour hair closer to Zuzi.

52

According to Mol, everybody has "problems," but Zuzi has only her "*problem*."

"You mean I'm mental," Zuzi says in a louder than usual voice. Mol shrinks back. For her it is a question of decorum.

"Your real name isn't even Zuzi, *Diane*," Mol whispers. "Like, you're as performance as I am. Only Zuzi could think of such a stupid thing. But I know Diane won't do it because, like, the very act of considering suicide makes it an essay question."

Mol sits back, slurping her salted caramel Frappuccino as if that has clinched her argument.

Zuzi looks away, sighs. Of course Mol is right. The whole thing is obviously a thesis: something to be developed in five tightly developed paragraphs. Definitely not like Nelly Arcan's novel, *Exit*. Zuzi feels ashamed.

She thinks about her sometime friend, Nik, who once every week goes to a place on Granville where they stick him with electric pins. He claims the electricity detoxifies the outside world's "reality poison" that has leaked into him.

"When I get out of there," he says, "I don't even care if it's raining. Or what the federal government is doing."

Drugs, she thinks. *My whole generation is addicted to popcult.*

Then she considers her baby. Sometimes when she goes home at night—her husband Marcus gone—she cuddles the cowgirl doll her mother brought back from Vegas. When she presented it, her mother said, looking very serious, "I won it *just* for you. In…*hopes*." And she'd emphasized the word "hopes" as if it were an incantation.

Every midday her mother wheezes and puffs through the machine exercises in the basement room of her old condo tower in Kerrisdale. Every night she smokes a big bong. "It's just so I can sleep. The smoke is more organic filtered through the water, y'know, Diane," she assures Zuzi. "I won't touch those filthy joints."

After the bong, she eats a large bag of Doritos Cool Ranch chips.

Zuzi sometimes dreams that the little doll she holds has come out of her body, that she has spread her legs one night and given joyous birth to her own girl who, as she is growing up, will refuse to learn to read because it will make her "more intellectually honest." Zuzi tells this future to the doll with straight-faced seriousness. She calls her daughter Lethis because she likes the sound this name makes when her tongue touches the bottom of her upper front teeth. Once Lethis is grown, they will together take on one world problem after another. They'll defeat the corporations, out-marvel Marvel.

As Zuzi tenderly addresses her, Lethis stares up at her mother, staring in wonder with her wide-open, round Hello Kitty eyes.

Everybody in Kitsilano under thirty-five has a dog, so she and Marcus decide to get one "sometime soon."

"He'll keep you good company when I'm out," he says, shoving his tongue down her throat as he kisses her goodbye.

Now she is all wet and he's gone. What to do?

She goes back to bed. But as she's staring at the ceiling and thinking about putting her hand under the covers "*down there*," in her mother's words, the phone rings. *Phone sex?* she wonders eagerly, then shrinks away from picking it up, embarrassed at the absurdity. *You're as bad as the rest, Diane.* But that begins the inching of depression back into her soul, so she flings the covers away, sits up straight, and answers.

"Jim Jarmusch here," she says in a soft American drawl.

There's a pause, a faint hiss of static, and she knows this means it's either God or a telemarketer.

"God?" she says. "Is that you?"

"Is Miss-USS di-Annee please?" an Asian-accented voice says, after some hesitation.

Zuzi feels a mean streak slithering inside, perhaps a product of the morning's unfulfilled tantric energy or a need to provide some friction against the smooth completion of the plans of the universe.

"This is Miss-uss *Zu-zi* Di-annee speaking," she says.

"Thanks to you," says the voice. "Please to consider talk about some free good credit cart issue for you."

"Godamnit I'll only talk to you if you can prove you're the Master Builder!" Zuzi says, "... or at least from God's office," she trails off sweetly.

There is more hissing and the sound of someone whispering not in English. Abruptly the phone clicks and there is silence.

Slowly, Zuzi puts it down. "Typical of God," she says and goes to meditate.

Later that morning she walks down Yew Street to Kits Beach. It's June and there is the usual lid of grey sky and a light drizzle that will last the whole month. But the lingering effects of the meditation lift it all away from her, as if she's shrugged out of a heavy jacket.

She thinks about getting the kind of dog she can take for walks around the inside of the apartment.

She thinks about getting a real doll, one that burps, whose diaper will have to be changed, who will grow up to say, "Fuck you, mom!" This makes her laugh to herself.

She thinks Marcus lives with her because she makes really good lasagna and needs sex. When he comes home, he likes asking her if she's "all right." She guesses this is a substitute for feeling something more. True, she does love to screw him. He *is* sweet. But his soul is so far away it might as well be in the Andromeda Galaxy. Sad and true. Now, they are both just another mutual dependency. Despondency. She is close to tears at the hopelessness of it.

But of what exactly? Who am I to doubt him? What can be changed and what can't?

And she thinks about Mol—the only person she physically spends real time with. Mol, who at least knows what it is to pay attention.

The others are cybermyths.

No, cybermoths, she thinks to herself, smiling a little. *Like doubts to a flame.*

Zuzi scuffs her shoe with sand that has been kicked onto the sidewalk by beach volleyball players. She looks up at the sky. Tiny raindrops poke at her eyes. Vancouver hums away in the background, all wound up going around and around. The ocean slops within a grey that goes all the way to Japan. Or at least Vancouver Island.

She remembers what Jim Jarmusch said: *Authenticity is invaluable; originality is non-existent.* And Jean-Luc Godard about imitation and stealing in art: *It's not where you take things from— it's where you take them to.*

Something gets through and whacks her hard on the head. She ducks too late. A black shape cursing in crow heads to the nearest tree. *Too close to the nest and their young, I guess. Well, they certainly have no doubts!*

She stops, squinting up at the blob of black now peering

with single-minded intensity at her from a nearby branch, ready to dive-bomb again. Struck by its fierce authenticity, she doesn't know whether to fight, run, or try to explain.

THE DUPLICITOUS DEAD

MAO

I turn off the cam, lean back in my chair, and ask Mao about the birds.

He looks at me with hesitant wonder, childlike—for just a second forgetting he's a god.

I saw the same look on Stalin's face as he was going over the edge.

"The sparrows," I say.

He doesn't turn to the interpreter but looks off into inner space. Then answers in soft, Mandarin phrases. Even before Mao is finished, the interpreter bows to me and says, "Every coin has two edges."

After this idiom clanger, I look at her carefully. Is she the same one who was there during the official interview or...? Hard to tell sometimes: ubiquitous cadre uniforms and short-chopped hair make superficial individuality difficult. At least for me. Come to think of it, the previous one might have been male.

"Pardon?" I say.

"According to the pertinent examples executed."

"Huh?"

"Their murdering is a case in point."

"I don't understand." But do, sort of. I'm hearing butchered phrases from ESL student essays, their magic formulas parroted to please whatever they think the bosses want. I used to read them for a living.

"The sparrows!" says the interpreter, impatient.

"Exactly. Well, what does he know about them?"

"All in all, that's why they are declared enemies of the state."

I know Mao ordered a China-wide massacre of sparrows because they were eating into the food "surpluses" of the next five-year-plan. In order to capture the evil capitalist infiltrators, obedient citizens grabbed their long nets and crossed rickety ladders stretched from roof to roof. I saw the massive sacks of dead birds hauled away. And the crammed cages of them let loose onto the killing fields, then blasted with machine-gun fire as they attempted to fly free.

Others were incarcerated with gangs of cats in massive prisons, or tortured by young boys specially trained to pull their wings off slowly. None of these sparrow traitors confessed in clear enough Mandarin to even make it to trial—they would have been convicted of treason anyway and summarily executed.

60

I think I am a child when this happens. I imagine I remember lying in bed alone, abandoned by my parents as they cavort shamelessly in their bedroom next to mine. I cry that childish cat cry because of their grunting pleasure, the dead birds, my punishing isolation.

"Moreover," the interpreter says.

"What?" I look at Mao as I say this. His public face is back on: unfathomable Buddha. Not for the first time I wonder if he's in the late stages of dementia. If I could slide behind that inscrutable round face, slightly open mouth, Mona Lisa smile...

Somewhere I still hope to find reality. But it seems like a mad pursuit.

"They always have the opinion one way and some of the others. All in all." The interpreter gathers up her papers and purses her mouth, still sexless.

"Wait," I say. "What happened next?" But I remember.

In the years following the massacres, insects multiply in their googol zillions and eat everything. This leads to mass famine. Millions die—Mao comforting a few of them by reading out of his Little Red Book, accompanied by his wife and Deng Xiaoping, of whom Mao says, "He is the saviour of the next generations." Deng who, after Mao's death, then betrays the Gang of Four including Mao's wife, burying Mao's legacy and thus helping to create the current corporate communist state party complete with Western-suited CEOs.

But that's much later.

After the famine starts, Mao turns his attention to bedbugs, who are declared allies of the yellow running capitalist dogs and pursued with merciless vengeance by the monomaniacal machinery of the People's state. Because everything is either on the side of the revolution—or not.

I watch him shuffle sadly away, surrounded by the mass dead, into a Glorious People's sunset.

And me? I feel my childhood rejections as sharply as if they're preserved in adamantine crystal. They're mine; I hold them jealously within. A terrible joy.

VIOLET

Grandmother is familiar with bedbugs. Spends her days at the hospital fumigating them out of the sheets. And mopping chemicals across the floors; swishing poison inside stained bedpans.

At night, Grandmother sits at home on a chair by the stove. Legs splayed wide, her head bends as she combs long red hair streaked with white. Looks up at me: quizzical, childlike. "Can't you turn that thing off? Good. Now let me show you a story."

I put the closed-up cam down. She points to the hologram opening like a flower in the middle of the shack's kitchen. "Watch!"

My young mother, still alive, blossoms within it; carefully bringing two basins of hot water, she lifts and places Grandmother's feet in each. "I remember when your gramma used to complain about her aching bones," Grandmother says to my mother, then sighs, wiggling her toes. "Pulling the plough through the mud on that old farm out in the bush. Your grampa'd try to make her drink whisky. She'd gulp a mouthful then spit it on the floor. 'You wouldn't need a wife if you could afford a mule,' she'd tell him."

"Oh!" My mother gets up quickly and backs against the sink. "I hear Dad!"

"Vio-let!" He slams against the rain barrel outside, stumbles into the screen door, falls through onto the clutter of junk in the dark, enclosed back porch. Staggers up and plants himself at the entrance to the kitchen, glaring.

"I'm a darkness," he says. "A rush of fire from The Black Watch. A terror."

"You're drunk," Grandmother says.

"Uh. Tell that to Walter Popoff."

Grandmother stands, her feet still in the washbasins. Hair drifts around her like midges caught in sunset-red above the town slough. She turns to my mother. "Go to bed."

"Don't—GO!" Grandfather whispers, lunges at her.

My mother squeals, bolts upstairs.

"Flighty." Grandfather shakes his head. "Was always…" His voice trails off.

"What did you do to Walter? Beat him up? The police going to be here?"

Grandfather waggles his finger, grows a crafty smile. "Let me tell you about the machine gun nest," he says, taking the drunk, straight walk to the kitchen table. "Explain everything."

"I've heard it. Ten thousand times. It's not '17 anymore. It's 1935. That was a long time ago. Why don't you go sit on the couch?"

"Oh no, oh no," he shakes his head. "You think if you get me to that couch I'll fall asleep for the whole night. I *know*… the things in your head, Violet. The way you try to…*move* me around. Try to make me *give* you things you can't give yourself."

Grandmother dries her feet off, puts on her slippers. "I'm tired. Put in a twelve-hour shift at the hospital. My bones ache."

"Hah!" He jumps up. "You sound just like your goddamn mother!"

"A mule."

"What?" He looks up at the stained ceiling of the converted grain shack that is their home, shakes his head again. "We didn't have no mules. Well, not up at the trenches. Back a ways. Bringing stuff in. Sometimes had horses." He falls back into a chair. "When the cavalry came. Early on before the tanks. Sent them against the machine guns. Don't know which was worse—horses screaming or men. All the blood got mixed up. We ate their mud blood. Begged that damned God to make the Boche miss. Bloody hell. Hardly ever missed."

"They missed you."

"No they didn't, woman! Didn't. Put a piece of shrap in my head. Metal." He thrusts a finger at his forehead.

"No one's ever found it."

"It's there, dammit!" His fist slams the table. Pause. Then he says quietly, "They'll find it. When I'm dead. You'll be sorry. Makes me do things."

His eyes get dark. Grandmother knows to say nothing, hold her breath, turn her eyes away.

"Want a drink," he says, childlike.

She gets up, makes a show of opening the cupboard, getting out some scotch, pouring it. He gulps it down and makes a face.

"Water! You put the damn water in the bottle. Tastes as much like scotch as my piss."

"You wanted a drink," she says.

"You're about as useful as the goddamn army, Violet." He jerks himself to his feet, stumbles back, looks down at his chest. "Some general with an Ontario smile pinned the metal on me."

"You mean *medal*."

"Sure. Metal medal. Said I destroyed a German machine gun nest. Single-handed. Don't remember a ting. Not a goddamn ting."

She knows he is dangerously drunk when he says "ting" for "thing." Cape Breton Scots bubbling up. Next he'll say "youse" for "you."

"What about Walter Popoff?" she says.

"Ah youse know...broken nose. Maybe an arm. Maybe a few ribs. Nuttin' much."

"Sweet Jesus!"

"Bloody Doukhobor wouldn't fight for his country."

"They don't believe in fighting. That's why they had to leave Russia. It's their religion."

Grandfather slowly rises. Walks carefully over, belts Grandmother hard in the face. She falls back onto the floor. Hair streaked with white. Red bubbling out of her nose.

The hologram shivers, winks out of existence.

"What is this bullshit?" I say to her after a moment of shock. "I saw you at the funeral, falling onto his grave and whining, 'Oh my poor Jim, they put metal in your head...they put metal in your head.'"

"*Sorry,*" she smiles. "*But I'm dead now too. And you know what? You can't really interview the dead.*"

TWO SISTERS

Yep, it's a problem. Once off the record, the dead don't tell you anything directly. Oblique at best.

But the rules are I can't interview the living. One consolation: the living aren't that reliable truth-wise either.

Right now I've got the two sisters sitting across from me. The interview's over so they're silent. Didn't say much during it either. Well, nothing in English, and I don't speak anything else.

After a long time in this white room, I notice the sign hanging around the neck of the one on the right—the skinny short one, gnarled like bark off an old poplar. It says, "Shawnadithit—Last of the Beothuks." She gifts a shy smile and raises her arms, wavering them slowly downward. Eyes locked on me.

We're abruptly enfolded in a Monet painting: intense cerulean blue overlaid with fat, drifting snowflakes: silent, mesmeric. I try to hear Debussy, but he and Monet are still in France. What gradually emerges out of the blue are the brittle bones of Appalachia, weathered and worn as they are here in Newfoundland and in northern New York, Scotland, Norway. Beneath them a river battering over rocks past scrags of pine and fir. A man stands there. Her father. I'm washed by an emotion I can't feel, sensing only the bleeding edges of something as far beyond me as Mars. He looks towards us, points. In slow-mo a bullet pierces his back: legs buckle, he lurches forward. No surprise on that face. A hatchet splits his skull, rubicund blood spattering cerulean and snow white. In the very next frame a ramshackle sawmill sits over the edge of the river, logs jammed across it, swamp spilling into the drowning forest.

With nowhere else to go, no other Beothuks left, Shawnadithit takes me to the white people's house in St. Johns. Who carefully, with infinite Christian love, feed her their civilized tuberculosis as I pretend not to record it.

Once again the white room. It stretches like the isolation zone in *THX 1138*.

I'm still trying to make sense of what just happened but I

see the other sister is nodding excitedly, recognizing the story. She too has a sign around her neck that reads, "Juana Maria— Last of the Nicoleño."

She rises, walks towards me, pointing at her feet. I look down and see footprints trailing away on the San Nicolas beach. She indicates I should follow her and I do. Seabirds screech overhead. The California sun is taffy-soft warm, and if I look carefully to the far southeast, on the mainland at San Clemente I can see Richard Nixon strolling barefoot on the beach. He waves. Pat waves. But Juana Maria is screaming at me in something that sounds like Aztec, so I reluctantly turn and follow.

She wants to show me her hut made out of whale bones. In front of it are blobs of seal blubber hung out to cure-dry in the sun. The blobs are black with flies. She also eats shellfish and any birds she can catch. A wild thing eating wild things. She smiles. Proudly alone for eighteen years.

She also lives in a cave when the weather is bad. We climb a short ways to it. The inside is littered with the bones of the native Alaskan otter hunters who had massacred the rest of her people, but who were then marooned on the island. Under the guise of feeding these aliens, she'd drugged them and cut their throats as they slept. Then drank their blood—claiming now to me in sign language that she was very thirsty.

I'm horrified at this. At the possibility of history being altered, creating a new and terrifying present. Even Mao did not have this power.

Hastily, I help her throw the bones off a nearby cliff into deep water, then get on the Internet and arrange for her to be rescued and taken to the Santa Barbara Mission where, safely imprisoned in 1853, she is dead seven weeks later from disease. Grandmother gets a huge kick out of all this. She turns to Mao sitting like a Buddhist statue beside her, his face frozen in that Mona Lisa smile of enlightened vacuity. "*You*," she says. "*Well at least you didn't kill them* all."

Then she faces me. I feel like I've been caught stealing cookies. Her smile is right on the edge. She says, "*You think your interviews—off the record or not—are about history. About a solid structure you live in. Like those old whale bones. You imagine you're here. Somebody else imagines you're not. Depends who's telling the story. It's that simple.*"

Then she laughs and laughs and laughs.

LOOKS LIKE
I GOT A
VULTURE

Of course no one notices the first one. It's by accident that I
do. But then my entertainment in this wheelchair is either to
stare into the TV or out the window. I prefer the window.

It's a rangy looking bird: long neck and ragged wings. Ugly.
Turkey vulture I think, but I'll have to look that up. It's
perched on the fire hydrant. All the years I've lived in this city
I've never seen such a thing.

What now? It isn't as if we haven't had our share of troubles.
First the earthquake. Then the riots. The Downtown Eastside
is still a mess: run-down apartment buildings and cheap new
condos collapsed in blood-spattered heaps. Which would make
sense for a vulture—especially since the city and the government are still arguing about who's going to clean things up. (I

notice they haven't mentioned the sleazy developers and why the city inspection department approved the crappy construction in the first place.) Plus there's been the recent deaths of our young men and women in that war halfway around the world. And of course there was the financial disaster when the corporate loan sharks they call banks defaulted on their debts to each other, throwing half the country's manufacturing plants out of business. Now there's no credit, no jobs, no savings. Finally, there are the Ponzi schemes running through town in the service of fantasy: leeches after blood, drawing from the poor what little money they have left.

I see on the news that many of the world's children are starving. But at least we're not shooting dissenters like they are in some of those religious countries—now, don't get me started on religion. My uncle always says about me, "Lighten up, eh." But he's got his swimming pool in the backyard, two BMW's in his garage, and a house in Hawai'i. I've got a miserable homecare worker and this disease.

I used to dream the aliens would show up and produce a miracle cure. Instead, looks like I got a vulture.

The next day I look out, and there are two more. Plus some additions lined up along the street. Kids are throwing rocks at them, but they hop away nimbly. Eventually the kids get bored and wander off. The vultures return.

I wonder if I should phone the SPCA, but that probably won't do any good. So I don't. Yet the birds make the news, spliced between a story on the latest pop star death from perpetual adolescence and a doping scandal in sports. By that time, these cadaverous things are all over the place. Someone emails the station calling them "Satan's Messengers." Okay...

The news stories are a confused mixture of sensationalism, science, and psychic mumbo-jumbo. One reporter describes the vultures as "out for blood." A biology professor opines that they have been driven into the city by a population explosion caused by global warming. A local astrologer says current planetary alignments haven't happened for several millennia and favour the appearance of "dark forces." An on-the-street interviewee offers that the vultures should be "like shot and we should, like, y'know go green an' use the meat for fertilizer in the parks. Or, y'know, give it away if the homeless are hungry."

Of course I think about that ancient Hitchcock movie. They never did figure out what made all those birds congregate and attack us, but for a long time I assumed it was Nature's revenge—until this wheelchair got me. Then I understood *life* is Nature's revenge. That was after my wife left; I was kind of depressed.

Usually I don't stay up at night. The dark haunts me. It's a place I might get trapped in.

But on a night several days after the first vulture appeared, I stay at my window, watching. The one on the fire hydrant in front of my house is still there. At least I think it's the same one, although it's hard to tell. It seems to be staring off into space, communicating—with Satan maybe.

Then something happens that frightens me. The power cuts out, and I sit in darkness. A hard moon appears above the house across the road, near the streetlight that normally obliterates it. Stick branches waver across my vision. And the vulture turns slowly until it is looking directly at me. I can't see its eyes at first. Gradually, however, I perceive a luminous bronze-gold pulse in the centre of each one. And I sense overwhelming intelligence. It's burning a message into my brain.

I panic, unthinkingly make the sign of the cross and somehow close the curtains.

The next morning I am still asleep when Cora arrives. She's my homecare worker, but that doesn't stop her from bursting into my bedroom and rasping at me, "Why are you still in bed?"

"Uhhhh," I say.

"Get up. The world's a mess."

I lurch onto an elbow. She has the top three buttons on her dress open. Jeez, that's the last thing I want to look at first thing in the morning. Cora's chest is a potential tsunami.

"So what's new," I say.

"The TV don't work. The radio don't work. The phone don't work—or I woulda called in sick. Lucky I live nearby. The kids next door says the Internet don't work, and they can't even play their Xbox. There's so many of them big, ugly birds everywhere I was afraida my life even walking this far. But I come anyway."

"Damn," I say. "There was something I was supposed to re-member about that. But it's gone."

"What do you mean?"

"Is the electricity back on?" I ask, not expecting to be that lucky, considering all the entertainment stuff doesn't work. So I'm surprised when she says, "Far as I know. Had a bacon and egg sandwich for breakfast. Fried up real good."

"Go make me some coffee," I say.

"Don't you be givin' me orders, mister."

"Cora. *Please* make me a cup of coffee. I'll get dressed and get in the chair. Maybe after I drink it I can remember."

She does as I ask. I'm sitting by the window when she

brings it, and I drink as we both look out onto the street. It's empty except for arguing vultures clustered around something squirming. Mine is still sitting on the fire hydrant, but it is turned away from me. Cora puts her hand on my shoulder. I take deep gulps of the hot coffee; its searing heat feels good going down my throat.

"What do they want?" she says, her hand now at the back of my neck, stroking it. That feels weird. I want to tell her not to touch me, but I'm also trying hard to remember what the damn bird said to me last night in my dream.

"I don't know," I reply. "If I could just think of it."

"Think of what?"

"Something...never mind. It's nothing. I must have imagined it."

"Well, I left my cellphone downstairs. I'm gonna go try it again. Maybe it works now, and I can call my kids. You want a bacon and egg sandwich?"

"Absolutely not," I say.

"Good. I'll make two and bring 'em up." She pats the mattress and winks at me. "We can eat together on the bed."

"Cora..." I say in exasperation, but she's already left the room.

While I wait, I let my mind go blank. I know the message is in there somewhere. Maybe it just needs to float to the surface.

But I have trouble concentrating because I'm distracted by Cora banging the frying pan and singing "Dream the Impossible Dream" off key. God, I loathe that song. There is even more noise when the thumping at the downstairs windows begins, then the breaking glass. I hear Cora's anger turn to shrieks of terror. Pots and pans are thrown around, but finally her screams and gurgling fade into silence. I wait.

Now I know what is squirming on the road and why all the windows are broken on the houses across the street. It's not rocket science; I just didn't want to see it. But I'm hyper focused now.

For some reason, I wasn't paying close attention. In fact, I feel like I haven't really paid attention to most of my life. I remember being sick—so long ago it now seems—smothered by the cloying love of my wife. I fought her off, desperate to run away. And it crippled me, so she was the one who had to leave.

Is it too late now? Can a cripple get uncrippled? I feel so sorry for myself and what I've lost.

When I roll the wheelchair over to the window, my vulture turns towards me. Those luminous eyes pulse shivers of gold even in daylight. I stare back, all attention. And then I remember the message. Of course. It's so obvious.

ORDINARY MADNESS

I awake suddenly. This often happens.

It's the combination of noise and quiet. The November moon, my white sun, is immense and silent, but the coyotes are hysterical beneath its light. Loopy, lupus. A friend of mine has it; she sometimes shakes wildly, says the pain in her body feels like a snakeskin she's trying to wriggle out of.

Tonight the cold calm sits on my skin in needle bites. I used to talk to it, my breath a plume of smoke. But everything I said was too loud; not talking helps me trust the silence.

I step naked onto cold linoleum floor. It feels like a slab of something dead. I'm rigid, think of warmth. Then don't think: feet into boots, throw on the coat, and head out the door. My body heat steams, melts a river through ground frost. Afterwards I'm shrivelled, shaking under moonlight burnt white behind a curling fog.

Am I safe here? I think of those German prisoners so many years ago in the internment camp not far from where the Cypress Hills forest rises out of prairie and where I get my wood. I've tried to find the exact internment spot, but the camp has been as efficiently disappeared as the Fascist atrocities it represented. Nevertheless the Germans of the Afrika Korps, far from Rommel and the dangerous palms of Tripoli, lived there in warm uniforms inside bunkhouses bright with light. Somewhere near Nichol Springs, a hollow in the hills. One calm night, snow falling, they listened on their one record player to Wagner's *Rienzi Overture*.

From Dresden, light years later, one of them wrote my uncle, who had been his camp guard: *"The music! It was a miracle for all of us! We have such tears in our eyes. It is the Fatherland! It is our liberation, our freedom!"*

My uncle replied with the following—and no comments— from the *Affidavit of SS-Obersturmfuhrer Rudolph Hess*, April 5, 1946: *"Children of tender years were invariably exterminated since by reason of their youth they were unable to work .... Very frequently women would hide their children under their clothes, but of course when we found them we would send the children in to be exterminated. We were required to carry out these exterminations in secrecy, but of course the foul and nauseating stench from the continuous burning of bodies permeated the entire area and all of the people living in the surrounding communities knew that exterminations were going on at Auschwitz."*

Back inside, I light the stove and kerosene lamp; inhale the thick-sweet smell of the oil. Kindling crackles into life. The moon is my sun, my morning. I'm trying to live in opposites. In the notebook, I carefully cross yesterday into today: November 11. Meticulous records must be kept to keep me from being disappeared. Will it snow today? Will they find me?

Before I check out the forest, I have a breakfast of brown rice and black beans. It's also lunch, supper, and tomorrow's breakfast. So it goes.

I have three things with me in order to survive.

Item #1: endless bags of the beans and rice. Mixed together, it's a complete food: all eight amino acids, balanced at 80% brown rice and 20% black beans. Like the blurb says: *Rich in complex carbohydrates, high in natural fibre and low in fat (with no cholesterol)*. The climate is dry; the mice easily satisfied. I immediately think of MacArthur Park in Los Angeles where I remember Eugene biting into his bratwurst, splattering grease from the burst end of it all over my face. His laughter, knowing I have to take it.

An interesting thing is happening: memory, imagination, and the outside world are breaking into something seamless, flowing. Einstein speaks ponderously from Eugene's massive black head: *"In a certain sense, therefore, I hold it true that pure thought can grasp reality, as the ancients dreamed."*

Sometimes I dream I awake suddenly. This often happens. Sometimes I am in Tujunga Canyon at the chicken ranch, the sweet stench of it as I wait, deep within the L.A. hills while earthquake aftershocks raise smoky dust. Brush fires burn away memory.

Item #2: *À La Recherche du Temps Perdu*. I use the English version, translated by Scott Moncrieff, that was given to me by a young woman whose name is on the inside cover. She writes: *"Dec. 10/92. With love, Your Lilyana."* I've heard nothing from her since and don't remember why she disappeared. There's an illegible signature beneath hers: '——————, *1941*,' and, inside, a bookmark from a used bookstore near

McGill in Montréal: *"Le Mot, 469, rue Milton. Où vous trouverez les meilleurs LIVRES D'OCCASION, Spécialisation: Littérature."*

Mysteries. Part of how and why I'm here.

Item #3: matches. Without heat I'd be dead. I'm no boy scout.

To get to the forest I step outside into what's left of the white sun. The prairie, now pressed beneath fog, is more flat than it really is. But infinite, which it is. Exactly like the inside of the Oratoire St.-Joseph in Montréal where French organ music—Vierne and Duruflé—gets me on my spiritual knees. Here I'm under a pregnant moon surrounded by ice crystals.

The coyote choral yapping will last until the yellow sun rises. When they stop, I become afraid. The clarity of daylight creates what can't be seen—the fear I fled here to avoid.

And so onto the trail behind the shack, past the outhouse, and down into the shadowed ravine leading back to the hills. How many times have I walked it? The absence of light is comforting. On the frozen mud, I stumble over tracks of mule deer: ears poised like megaphones as they look up, hesitate in my mind, then lope off to the horizon. Fall off the other side, probably.

Every day I read Proust until I come upon something to record, invent. It's a long or short process, depending on whether or not I recognize within me any symbols from the outside world. He writes: *"... I should, no doubt, have longed to see and to know it, like so many things else of which a simulacrum had first found its way into my imagination. That kept things warm, made them live, gave them personality, and I sought then to find their counterpart in reality, but in this public garden there was nothing that attached itself to my dreams."*

But now I flinch when my boot breaks through thin ice, slaps water, sticks. It pulls out with some effort, sucking air. The ravine has widened, the creek here a slough. The white sun is gone, and the east is becoming yellow. A short way ahead there are trees with snow frosting on top. I see German soldiers amid the Christmas trees, eating plum pudding and singing "O Tannenbaum," ecstatic to be out of Afrika and into a Black Forest cake.

When I reach the top of the first hill, I pause and look behind. Far to the south, smoke trails thinly from the shack. Glacier-rounded mounds break from grey wool into a hint of sunlight; near the horizon, there is the flat gleam of Pakowki Lake. But still I scan for them; even now they may be trailing me like a pack of demonic wolves. It's because of the country, the imagination it creates. Space demands meaning and morality. If you're going to live in it, you have to deal with whatever you bring in your pack. The problem is to find the conditions of trust. Proust: *"What criterion ought one to adopt, in order to judge one's fellows? After all, there was not a single one of the people whom he knew who might not, in certain circumstances, prove capable of a shameful action."* A condition producing either paranoid liars or people who help each other. I'm caught in the middle.

Ergo: what I am doing here is absurd. Like the hockey game we played on the irrigation reservoir southwest of Medicine Hat when I was thirteen. Its only boundaries the ice half a mile long and one hundred yards wide. Any number on your team. No goalies. You have to pass the puck every twenty or so strides (nobody counts). Offside is a pass to someone skating beyond the last defensive player. No time limit. Sometimes there's a week between periods; sometimes there are ten periods. One score ends 87-74. After a day *"out there,"* as my father would say, you sleep dead.

Sometimes my dad comes to watch me play. Now in a sharp cut of memory I miss him. Again look behind me. Shouldn't. I'm trying to learn not to imagine the past I fear.

When I first got here, I asked around and was directed to a middle-aged rancher who said she had a shack, far out into her rangeland, in which it was "possible" to live.

"Used to be the sheepherder's when my brother tried runnin'm." She looks me straight between the eyes. "So you wanta be alone." She makes it a statement.

"Yep."

"Really alone."

"Definitely."

"You come to the right place. There's a well. Water ain't so hot but it'll keep you alive. A stove. You can get wood from the Cypress Hills—the west end's inside my property. You'll have to chop and haul it. Oh. If you're gonna die, do it in winter so you'll stay froze until I get you out in the spring."

"I don't have to worry, eh?"

"About what? Dyin'?"

"People."

She shrugs. "Mostly I'd worry about what's in here." She taps her head. "On the other hand, you never know what's on the other side of them hills. Watch your back." And she winks. "Me. I'm off to Hawai'i, but I won't cancel the phone...in case you wanta haul your ass all the way back here and call home. Anyway, the boys'll be around now and then."

"I don't have a home. I don't want a phone, boys around."

She shrugs again. "Whatever. There's only one rule: I don't want no cops out here. For any reason." She stabs her finger. "No! Cops!"

80

Echoes of L.A. That was my line: "No cops, man."

But you want the money, you do business with who has it, who runs it. The stuff comes through the pipe at Tijuana, up the aqueduct to the Mexicans on Sunland Boulevard, the parking lot of the *Pollo Loco Restaurant* to be exact. Then individual distribution from the chicken ranch in Tujunga Canyon. My share I hauled, via a slow bus ride through La Cañada Flintridge, to the Galleria in Glendale where I made the delivery to a bunch of Suits over Chinese noodles in the Food Fair. I could smell Simi Valley all over them: they were nervous without their boots, patrol cars, hip guns, dark glasses.

"It's for the pension fund," one of them smirked.

From the Cypress Hills I survey the wide world.

Proust tells me: *"Our hands do not tremble except for ourselves, or for those whom we love."* Late morning sun shines weak dishwater through these shaky fingers.

Inside the pines I'm a shadow. Near the forest edge, thick twisted lodgepoles cluster uneasily, bent east. Farther up they are thin, closer together, and would be sighing if there was wind sifting through them, but even up here on this rare day they barely move.

I trek hard. Stop at an overlook, curl in a hollow and stare. The prairie is a Rorschach; I see a last vision of my family. And the drug rock 'n' roll ride after we had run all the way to Montréal to hide. Children crying, wife angry, *"Why are we here?"* Me on manic streets, in demonic Métro, upon mad Mountain, *"Why am I here?"* Oldest son's laser eyes: *"You promised to be the kind of father you said you'd be!"* Words blazed into metal spiderweb Pont Champlain.

As each of them fades, atom by atom, I awake suddenly. This

often happens. I'm sure they have found me, or the ones I love are near again. Frantic, look for mercy: someone who'll forgive me. But the world in my eyes is just water, a blur.

Then, inexplicable as a dream, I'm back in the shack of cold dark morning. Beans and kerosene smell of Proust lying trapped in his room. Even here his paper words burn: *"How often is not the prospect of future happiness thus sacrificed to one's impatient insistence upon an immediate gratification."*

At the touch of a match I watch them grin and curl.

Yet there are days of gifts. They come simply: days when I'm not pursued, instead am here beyond time and worry, in a miracle I don't deserve. Winter held beyond the horizon. A yellow sun almost warm.

I step into the land, feel I'm made for it. Peace drifts out of blue sky, rises from dry earth. I leave the shack, stride plains, climb barbed wire, cross empty sloughs of matted weeds, bulrushes. See sparrows, distant cattle, a fleeting herd of pronghorn antelope strung across the next hill. And within prairie space redolent cow, deer, coyote, and antelope plop; sharp tang of dried wildflowers. No humans. With each foot I put forward, strength wells through me. I become a burning tree, a writhing snake, a crazy coyote. I am the fire-twisted prophet, a universe of one. I move over the ridge where glacier-dropped rocks sit like arrows. Pointing to the other side.

I'M NOT BUYING YOUR LIES ANYMORE

Mel looks up as the sky cracks open. Blood oozing through and across the dome of it: fat red drops.

No one notices. It's expected.

She stomps into Suli's apartment, shaking the drops from her.

"Shit! Don't do that on my carpet," he says, then sees her face. "What happened?"

"Nothing. Blood shower."

"Oh," he shrugs, turns away. "You infected again?"

She goes to the sink, washes her hands. "Don't think so. Should I go to the hospital?"

He shakes his head. "*They* won't do anything. I was there this morning. Psych ward's full."

"Who?"

"Today it was oil execs, couple of politicians, some bankers, and military. Oh. And a hockey player, an NFL quarterback, and a nurse."

"They give you anything?"

"Some dope, Molly, case of beer."

"Uh."

"You want some?"

"I like being sane."

"Yeah, right." He twists his mouth in that cute look he has.

Covertly, she looks over his smooth, naked chest. Remembers what's under that disguise. But there's a sudden drumroll and smash of cymbals. Flash of strobe lights through the windows.

"Blood shower must be just about over," Suli says. "Look, Mel. If you're not going to take anything with me you should fuck off. I don't know what I might do if you turn into something dangerous."

"You're right. I'm gone."

She slinks home, taking the middle of the road that no one drives down anymore. There are flashes of darkness in the sidestreets, but there is no way she's going there. Darkness is not always good.

At home—her door double locked—she pours herself a forbidden glass of water then grabs the knitting needles. At their touch it's a flash to her mom and the time she noticed the little lines first appearing above her mother's upper lip. The signs before they took her away.

Mel was the one who called it in, before she knew better. She shivers, remembering her mom crying, her head against Mel's shoulder as they put on the restraints.

"I will *never* abandon you," her mother hissed in her ear, wet tears running down the side of Mel's face.

She twists her hair at the memory; blaze of pain behind her eyes. Memories are dangerous. Like shadows. Things hardly there but they can still ambush. Or it could be withdrawal from what they euphemistically call "life support." She takes a gulp of the water, then looks at it suspiciously.

It's hard to know what to think.

She sits down and begins. The knitting needles move swiftly, knitting the air. There's been no wool since her mother left, but the action gives Mel the feeling that her mom hovers over her like a shadow; the soft touch of her ambivalence presence enough.

The next day there is a party. It is being hosted by The Coalition to End Coalitions. Members of the media are there mostly because they are running for office. A prominent member of the PMO arrives fashionably early, accompanied by a woman from the NSA and an attractive man who claims to play centre forward for Essendon in the Australian Rules Football League. Mel allows her eyes to caress the latter's perfectly proportioned frame, especially his wide shoulders and narrow waist.

Mel has come with Ella and Suli. They babbled the whole way about the need to reinstate the one-child policy because there are too many people in their apartment. It was a difficult conversation. The three of them had embedded themselves in a Start the War parade and along the way there was considerable interaction between it and the military, who were bent on keeping the current peace. After dodging several casualties resting in the middle of the road, Mel managed to shout at Suli, "We never had a one-child policy! That's China!"

"What do you know about China?" Ella had shouted back. "Have you ever been there?"

"No!"

Suli added. "Don't go! The McDonald's in Shanghai is terrible!"

"I hate McDonald's," she'd muttered.

Mel is not a fighter. She remembers Laura and Dell, her two dearest dolls from when she was four. She remembers that war: how Dell sawed off Laura's head and Mel had to help Dell bury Laura's head and body in the backyard because the shadows were prowling and her mother wouldn't let them go over to the empty lot behind Walmart.

That was the day her father disappeared.

Now she shrugs her shoulders. The AFL player interprets this as rejection and quickly shifts his eyes back to the woman from the PMO. Mel notices only obliquely. The speeches for the evening have temporarily abated and everyone else is getting blasted on the oxygen that's being passed around.

She slumps into a corner, suddenly exhausted. Jairo slides down beside her.

He's apparently Spanish, but his English is impeccable. He once told her he'd been directly "translated" to North America.

"I don't know what that means," she'd said.

He had given her a wry smile. "It's a yoke, a transatlantic yoke. Everyone knows how 'j' is pronounced in Spanish."

Now she looks at him. "You're not going to tell any more yoke-jokes are you?"

He shakes his head. "I'm getting old. Look at the grey hair in my beard. I can't take these funerals anymore."

"Funeral? I thought this was a party about politics."

"Speaking of funerals." He inches closer to her. "I think I know where your father is."

Something slides around inside her; something she thought she'd chopped away long ago. A deep cut. Then it's gone just as abruptly. She grabs the oxygen bottle with its mask attachment and takes a deep drag.

"You alright?"

"No."

"Okay. Do you want to find out?"

"Yes."

"You have to go to the Costco in Ebola. I'll tell you exactly where inside the store. *If* you can make it there." He smirks.

Mel looks at him. Ebola is a dangerous part of the city, full of unpredictable rich people.

"Before I go," she says, "have you been to the psych ward lately?"

He shakes his head. "Suli convinced me I don't need that anymore."

"But everyone goes."

He gives her a wry smile. "I notice *you* don't go."

"Um," she says. "I'm just on water now."

She takes Suli with her. The crack in the sky has been fully sealed by the time they get to the Costco supermarket.

Suli points upwards to the round sun that has already been

reattached. "That was fast. The work crews must've been up all night."

"Who gives a shit, as long as they do their job. Hardly anyone does anymore."

"My, my," Suli says. "Somebody's feeling just a little too good this morning. Although I know you don't like the sun."

She glares at him but doesn't answer.

The Costco door is wide open. Beyond the building, the giant castles of Ebola loom over the squat warehouse. Inside Costco, the shelves are only half-filled with bodies.

"Where is everyone?" Mel says.

"It doesn't matter. I don't need a banker to show me. Jairo told me where he is."

There are shadows at the back of Costco. Mel knows she has to go there. Why hasn't she visited him before? She shakes her head, shivers, leaves Suli, who is still looking for the missing bodies.

She is soon enclosed in darkness, as if the living world has ceased to exist. *He* encloses her.

"I know what you did to me," she breathes.

There is a moment where the darkness shifts. Then his voice, mellifluous: "No, you don't. You're wrong, wrong about everything."

"That's a lie," she says. "I've watched you take over...your fascism hidden behind a corporate promise to protect. Paranoia so you can have more powers to snoop and spy, to feed on your own. To turn your family against itself, one against the other. To destroy any climate of trust and sustenance. I watched my pathetic mother internalize that so she ate away at herself. You've made the world into something to fear, to need to escape from."

"You never loved me," he says. He seems to be crying. "You believed everything from the outside and nothing from the inside where you know the truth is. I didn't craft that image. It's not what I really am."

"Then *show* me!" she screams at the darkness.

Behind her, she hears Suli yelling her name. He's clearly panicked. "They're coming from the castles! The rich are coming!"

But his voice recedes into a meaningless buzz, reverberating and overlapping so it sounds like all the voices in the world are merging into incoherence.

The darkness opens, becomes a knife of light. Her father descends, his arms spread wide to embrace her. "I'll show you," he says, his deep voice full of caring authority.

Perhaps this is just another blood shower. On the other hand, a perverse part of her wants him, wants him so desperately. The heat of it. She is frozen in fear and indecision.

"I know," he says, with infinite patience. "I understand. It's hard to know what to think."

But then she remembers. He's always said this. It was always his excuse: the easy way out. Fear and then paternalism.

Mel looks at the vast Costco warehouse, all the shiny pills it sells, the lines of the Ebola rich surging down the aisles towards her. She smiles a sad smile. But also shakes her head. "No, dad. I'm not buying your lies anymore."

THE BIG ROOM

ZED

"*Breasts*," Noll says to me, putting down her phone to stare at the grey on the other side of the window.

I get up painfully, move to the huge sheet of paper on the wall. Carefully check off the appropriate box.

"*We're alone. Each of us. Separate.*" I read it out loud although it's in bright-red block letters up there at the top of the sheet. My voice wavers.

"As if I didn't know." She's crying as she says it, so I move over to touch her shoulder. She pulls away a millimetre but it's enough.

The huge monitor on the far wall facing us plays silent news from Gaza: the Israeli Defense Forces have blasted a U.N. school and the distraught parents are carrying small bodies into the street. People have their mouths open, faces twisted. Wailing, I'd guess.

She nods towards it. "Jews acting as World War II Germans does nothing to inspire me about the human race."

I wait half a minute. Then say, "You're hitting back because you're Jewish. Victimizing is an act of revenge."

But I'm being perfunctory—it's our old routine. And, as usual, she refuses the bait.

One of the phones rings and rings. She answers, relays the info, I tick them: *Brain, Prostate, Colon, Duodenal, Stomach*. Then I say, "Busy out there."

"You mean God."

"I don't know anything about Him/Her/It/Them."

"What did you say about revenge?"

After a long silence while she clicks through the world's horrors, she says, "By the way, the '*Breast*' one was my sister."

What can I say to that? I shrug. I'm pretty sure she doesn't see me. There's enough space in this apartment—we call it The Big Room—that you can hide small things.

We work hard through the afternoon, adding items to the categories.

Sometimes it's difficult filing correctly without a clear diagnosis. What do I know about these things? *Heart* could have been caused by *Brain*.

But we have no choice. Towards evening I struggle to my feet—the hip feels like a steel shaft is twisting through it—and haul myself over to the window. The sun has come out but we're in shadow, which is fortunate because now there is bright, angled sunshine drowning the nearby ocean, palm trees, and surrounding apartment buildings in a wash of light. Looks a lot like Waikiki so I try to find Diamond Head but it's not there. We're somewhere tropical though.

Wish we could go outside, I think. Not for the first time.

Then I notice there's something ugly happening down on the street. Looks like the police are busting up the homeless shelter in the nearby park again. They clear it out every few weeks and then it gradually sprouts back again like a fungus, covering up the bird shit until there are mushrooms of dirty tents everywhere.

Smoke bursts from canisters. Shots are being fired—I can tell from the way the bodies jerk like puppets before they fall. Opening the window's forbidden, so this happens in silence. A ballet. And that is the frustration for both of us: real life takes place outside. Why have we been shut inside The Big Room? Why does no one return our calls?

Even more strange is how—like magic—they are able to get invisibly by us every night to deliver the crap food we're forced to eat. The endless fried chicken, taco salads, bags of chips, Nanaimo bars, and cans of Coke have made us huge; she can't even move through the apartment without her motorized chair. The pulley system I have to use to get her onto the toilet is ridiculous. And I can barely hobble with this hip pain. There's no space between my thighs, and the skin sores have me constantly trying to scratch my balls, which I can barely reach. Haven't been able to see anything down there for quite a while.

Also haven't voted since they put us in here. How long? Years and years, I think. She says it's some kind of experiment, as if that explains or justifies it. On the other hand, there was that letter a while ago from the police thanking us for "helping" them with their "inquiries."

Every wall in this apartment—except for the one with the sheet of paper covering it—is filled with gigantic monitors showing the news on Internet sites. At first we wouldn't watch because it's terrible: things you don't want to know or be reminded about. But after a while what else is there to do? Oh yeah, you might get interested in something happening outside the window but then they switch it. For example, right now I can see a studio and the Prime Minister is playing rock 'n' roll on the piano. His dog is beside him. A hockey stick leans against a nearby wall. To message his cool, he's wearing an open-necked shirt—or is that an Ivy League sweater?

I'm so old my gag reflex brings up Pat Boone, Richard Nixon, and Up with People.

The Big Room is deceptive. In the part we're working in now there's enough space for all the monitors, computers, and other electronic junk I don't know how to use. Off to the side is a kitchen. And down the long hall a bathroom and three bedrooms (one we sleep in and the other two filled with boxes and boxes of old toys and exams from our school days). The walls, when you can see them, are a dirty white. Makes me wonder who lived here before.

I used the word "deceptive" because sometimes The Big Room is frighteningly claustrophobic: a tiny space crammed with objects. At other times it seems to swell until it feels infinite: I look down the hall and there's no end in sight. Terrifying.

The answer is to never look too closely, to keep working.

We send emails everywhere. It says they've gone through, but we never get replies. On top of that, if we don't fill out the sheets of paper (when they're complete they're somehow changed for blank ones—probably in the middle of the night) we don't get food. I could sure use some hot wings and a big taco salad right about now.

I remember when I was young. I had big ears and a short

haircut. I was so skinny I had trouble keeping my pants up and my belt tight. I went to church and thought nothing of it.

NOLL

I want to pee again.

Well, actually, I don't, but I'm hoping after Zed lowers me onto the can I can send him back into the living room so I can be alone long enough to have a good cry.

Crying is my exercise. Unless you count breathing.

At first I'm thinking it's about my sister. Then I think, no, it's probably all those other cancer deaths that come at us. But I know it's partly about Mahmoud. Maybe it *is* just exercise, yet it has triggered me to think about him. Those memories never bother Zed; he's at the window, as usual, mesmerised by the outside.

Mahmoud is a strange story in our life. How we got him in particular. I think I remember it correctly.

There was a mysterious phone call from what they said was the "Child Displacement" office. They had this refugee kid from somewhere in the Middle East—could have been Palestine. But there was some murky political background to it. Or my guilt. Or maybe somebody's idea of a "reward"?

But we got him. He was so cute! Little button nose, thin body, and a sweet mouth full of English words even though anyone could see he was Arabic. Yet strange blue eyes and a wonderful smile if you could get it to work.

I was young then. Thinking about it again now, after so long, I'm sure it was guilt. Yes, punishment.

Just before we got him, I'd been a sniper for the Americans. Black-on-black ops. Young, Canadian female volunteer: ponytail and wide-eyed makeup; fake passports and embassy clearances. Newlywed. Zed and I had met in bed so we could get the formalities over with. And all of it worked. Theatre of the absurd.

I know it sounds ridiculous. But they told us the more ridiculous the better. We got in and out of countries wearing our innocence like an invisible uniform.

No one paid much attention to me. I was skinny and could scoot down narrow alleys, climb twisted stairwells, and thread my way across cluttered rooftops while Zed leaned against brick walls, the tourist smoke trailing out of his nostrils as he wore that *I'm-so-impressed-by-the-local-architecture* look. And I was way more efficient than some fat-ass drone—created less media blowback.

I learned to be invisible. After taking delivery, I'd "feed the *baby*"—that's what we called it. And I loved it. There is nothing more satisfying than being intimate with your tool the way I was: lining up *baby* through the sights, caressing *baby* with it—the way God feels when he locks onto us, yet no way we know He's there.

I especially liked feeding a mother, a daughter. Always more effective in the long run, pushing the protecto buttons the husbands/fathers carry in their emotional backpack: their despair when they fail. At the same time I felt I was liberating other females from their playtime vacuity in the world of men. It often made me think of my mother after the silencer pop, the slight recoil as the *baby*, in its part of the dance, threw itself backwards... that one magic second before anyone else knows the laws of the moral universe have been broken yet again.

My mother. What did she think when this girl baby popped out? I wondered why she had me.

Mahmoud was the punishment I asked for as a reward. When I wanted to be a mother myself. But that was later, when the psychopathic distance disappeared.

ZED

We emerge from the tunnel at HarbourFront station.

I could have chosen the previous stop, Outram Park; we could have walked a ways, and climbed a high hill in the sweep of warm rain drifting across Singapore, then taken a gondola across to the island. But Noll wouldn't have it. She hates get-ting wet, and she doesn't think it's safe. In her old age she's become very careful about imagining reality. Well…me too, if I'm being honest.

Once, we really were in Singapore. It's out the window of The Big Room now.

I can see myself leaving the subway, climbing up the stairs and getting Noll one of those small wieners in a bun they sell everywhere there. She can still walk at this point but she's slow. After I bring her the hot dog, she flops into the nearest chair and asks for three more. I don't have the hip problem yet, so I get them.

"Well?" she says after I settle myself. She stops eating and looks at me.

"Well what?" I say, uncomfortable, knowing what she wants to talk about.

"What d'you mean, 'well what?' What did you think of the execution?"

"Oh…I kind of enjoyed it, far as that goes. But I think he was drugged. There wasn't that much to see. They tie them up tight so they can't kick their arms and legs, and they drop

97

them so far it breaks their neck right away. Kind of makes it anticlimactic. But I like the idea they use executions as entertainment here."

Early that morning, as part of the mini tour we were on, we'd gone out to Changi Prison to watch someone get hanged who'd been caught smuggling drugs. I was hoping it would turn out to be an interesting outing, help take our minds off trying to get around in this terrible humidity and tropical heat. At least it was air-conditioned where the audience sat.

She sighs and looks away, then turns back towards me. "And you think hanging that young Australian boy—he was twenty-one years old for god's sake—will now stop people from trying to smuggle drugs." She says it as an accusation.

I shrug. "I dunno. Maybe. The government here thinks so."

"I can't stop thinking about Mahmoud."

"That's different. You should stop doing that."

"I can't."

Panic sweeps through me. If she ever finds out I helped turn him in to CSIS—who then handed him over to the Americans—I'll lose her forever. My knees are weak. There's a sudden pain lancing through my hip. She remembers what we did when we were young, how I reacted to it, but I don't want to.

I can't lose her. I can't. I can't.

NOLL

There was a long period that was basically blank: we went here, we went there; we made money, we lost it. We treated those we cared about with consideration and love; we treated them like shit. I don't know where all the decades went. We seemed to be living in the outside world inside an abstraction, a cloud.

Maybe I shouldn't be saying this here, but I lost interest in sex with Zed a long time ago. Still, I have to admit that once in a while I feel a twinge of interest when he has a certain look about him in his eyes, a bit of movement in his hips.

Somewhere in the middle of all this Mahmoud appeared. Where do children come from anyway? Take your choice, I guess: God, straight biology, found under a bush. I thought I remembered the story correctly—what I said before—but now I'm not sure.

I think he was adopted. I thought it was my reward to assuage my guilt. It was a long time ago.

Zed wasn't wild about him. Maybe that's when I lost interest in sex. Sex is about life. Children are about life and life is always about the future. So how could I think about a future with Zed if he couldn't see one for himself? I'm sure he thinks now that his life has been successful, but that's pure delusion—and selfish. He thinks about success as personal, in a way that thinking about the future of life isn't.

Well the kid turned out to be Muslim and that didn't go over too well in the North America of the time. But I loved the way he went into the world as a young adult: strong and clear. He had the courage I never had. Meanwhile Zed was already at the stage where he was dependent on me for *his* life. Truth is he's forever locked into the present. I'm going to die one day. Which is why he can't think about the future.

I've noticed a lot of men are dependent on women for their emotional existence. But there's more to it with certain kinds of them. I'm thinking about the ones who don't OD on their testosterone, that is. The leaders of the pack push into the competitive world, arm-wrestle each other—maybe that's a kind of anti-procreation animal sex—beat up women or use them as an audience, then get weak and die. All so they don't have to feel what it means. Zombie awareness.

The pack leaders are useful to us only for extracting their resources—energy and money. Well, and the odd masochistic pleasure. But the weaker ones, like Zed, are the ones women can actually live with.

Mahmoud, on the other hand, was a rare young man who would not approach anyone unless the interaction was about sharing. You can't truly share with someone unless you can offer naked self-knowledge. So first you have to get some. That is itself a kind of strength. Independent women love a man like that. I loved Mahmoud.

Somehow the neocon libertarians got the idea he was a "terrorist"; at that time, terrorism had taken over from "communist" as the main tool of the ruling class to manage the rest of us.

I've always suspected Zed. I think he helped them concoct evidence so they could take Mahmoud away. In those days all the nations of the West were hell-bent on using "terrorism" to install a sub rosa government. The oil corporations in particular were happy to give their support. Zed had strong connections to Bay Street and Wall Street then, before he lost everything.

He thinks I don't suspect him. Well, understandable. He's completely forgotten that other life when I was an assassin for those very same governments and corporations. And he's forgotten *his* connections to that establishment.

Once in a while, when I think about Mahmoud, I think about using my old skills on Zed. But what's the point. We're both trapped here in The Big Room and everything that happened back then is locked outside.

I hate him for that.

ZED

Noll has led a sheltered life.

I've worked hard to give her the support she needs and to protect her from the anxiety that can overwhelm her if she knows too much. I think that's what a good partner does: you try to compensate for her weaknesses and she compensates for yours.

Maybe she has too much imagination now and then, but I'm glad she's not the adventurous type. In that sense, our life together has worked out fairly well. I can't think of anyone else I'd rather be locked up in The Big Room with.

Some of what I've done in the past I've been able to keep inside. It's a good thing even those closest to us can't look straight in, see what's really there. Thank god there's no window into the soul.

I walk over and look outside once more. It's blank. Must be a change of scene coming. I wonder what they'll throw up next. And speaking of next, I'm also really curious to see what our ensuing category will be when we get back to work. *Dementia? Rare Pathologies? Moral Dilemmas in the Age of Disbelief? Therapy Lying?*

On the giant wall monitors, a man is being set on fire.

I'd better get Noll out of the bathroom. She must be finished and feeling all alone in there.

WELL, YOU COULD CHANGE YOUR LIFE

On the corner of Hastings and Main she awakes, frozen. Unable to decide. She's staring across the street at what is then a post office gleaming in spring light, her back to the Carnegie Library. Groan of the city around her. She has no idea what to do next, overwhelmed at how almost every action she's taken to accomplish something has put her on this corner.

Later she sees she was lucky. She could have been swept up by passing Gospel Mission scavengers, Conservative Party hacks, covert CSIS/CIA operatives, slumming executives, or drug pimps. Even a persuasive serial killer could have had her.

Instead, a man, mostly toothless, dirty beard and patient eyes amid traffic of machines and people, immediately recognizes where she is, faces her, some kind of bird squawking above his head.

"It's not as bad as you think," the saint says softly. "Caught against a rock. Push off a little, the current'll take you again. I know." He smiles, waves a dirty finger, disappears into the crowd.

She immediately hikes twenty blocks back to her basement suite, desperate for some candy, desperate to call Megs, Ken, Shia, Andria, anyone. But they won't answer. Instead she takes the only other recreational drugs immediately available: television and then sleep.

Ten years earlier she is living in a gentrifying NDG Montréal neighbourhood off Monkland: a row house that has bones of brick and dark wood and luminous oiled floors. She has chosen all her furniture, meticulously instructed by her husband's mother.

In the daytime she sits inside in the quiet, listening to the old clock, waiting for a baby to appear inside her. Sometimes she goes out to the backyard and pulls her dress above her knees in the sun. One day, emboldened by the heat of pulsating light, she pulls it higher, showing her "solid thighs" (her mother's words). There is a West Indian man doing carpentry work on the house opposite. She notices him looking at her and fingering himself inside his pants, and it gives her mild adrenaline for a while. But that passes.

For several months, once a week, she takes the bus to the Villa-Maria Métro station, rides the Orange Line to Lionel-Groulx, and then transfers to the Green Line, getting off at

Atwater where she walks the underground link into Dawson College. Here she sits through lectures on "Greek Women of the Islands," delivered by a young instructor who has bulging muscles and an ugly moustache. She has trouble looking at him. More often than not she retreats to the college library where she stares at the cross hung on the north wall, a reminder that this was once the Mother House of the Congrégation de Notre-Dame. Perhaps it's a message that books are to be used for fantasy. Given the stories in the Bible, she finds this comforting.

At night after supper, she and her husband watch cricket, hockey, rugby, soccer, baseball, tennis, football, darts, poker, etc. Oh, and Home and Garden Television. They have never spoken much. At first, this appearance of familiarity gives her a sense of romantic security, an enclosing peace she did not know in childhood. Then she thinks of how he cums almost right after he enters her, whenever she makes any kind of movement or sound.

Once she used iron control, made herself a robot. He thrust at her long enough for her to fantasize to the point where she could hold back no longer and gasped deep in her throat as the tidal rush lifted to throw her forward. He came and withdrew just as the wave broke.

She also wants to talk to him about why he joined the Conservative Party, and why he practises his bad French so intensely these days. But he just sits there. The television score is love-40. The couple decide not to sell even after the incredible makeover.

Of course, we are young, she thinks. What else is there to say? It will be different in a few years.

When she finally has the child, nascent possibility often seems enough for her to construct a future—very easy when her daughter is a three-year-old but much more work at sixteen. However, the good thing is that time passes and soon she is alone again.

Somehow she has left her husband at one of the stops along the way. Occasionally he phones, but there is just the familiar silence. He sometimes comes up in conversations she has at the group.

"Do you feel any differently about him now?" Catherine says, her white hair framing her round, smiley face. "Now that you've been on your meds for so long and on your own."

She shrugs. The others wait for her answer, anticipating—the caring emotional vultures they can't help but be.

"Well. I was alone long before he left, or I left him. Guess it really depends on your perspective of who's moving away from whom."

They nod, mildly perplexed at her complexity and her grammar.

"That's what I was just saying to my wife, the other day," Randy jumps in, enthusiastic. "My son won't talk to me and had me up on those charges…and of course I know I have health issues but I have to set boundaries, and I told him, I told my wife, I says, I'm not going to answer the phone or talk if he's swearing and carrying on, especially when he's refusing to take his medication all these years, and I just know, I have to tell you, how I'm upset about our granddaughter and what he might do, and I told my wife just yesterday that I said to the police when they came that they'd have to do something, but that's another story and—"

"Of course it is," Catherine's soft voice breaks in. "Of

course, and you've set boundaries. You have to look after your-self or you won't be able to look after anyone else."

She hears Catherine's words bounce around inside her head. How do you learn "to look after yourself" (*look after your-self until there's joy*)? She has asked that question and received lists. Checklists. One tick on the paper, one tick at a time.

It is why she likes to go home after the meetings and sit in the dark and listen to the ticking of her ancient clock.

Her friend Samji tells her people don't know how to look after the Earth.

"How can they look after Earth if they can't even look after themselves?" she says with unshakeable conviction in Hindi accented echoes of British English. "Here's my list: vars, rapes, starvation, torture, slavery, and now the spectre of complete environmental disaster. Ve have no long-term thinking, just short-term indulgence. Ve are like children who grew up vithout the parents. Enlightened self-interest so completely beyond us. Ve can't even realistically plan next generation. Our children appear from novhere and disappear into it. And reli-gion. Don't get me started on it!"

Everything Samji says seems cutting-edge accurate to her. She can feel the slices right across her soul. *It is happening.* She feels it, feels it as something incomprehensible, way beyond tears. The beginning of fulfillment maybe, but that is so far down the road it is still invisible.

When she watches television, it is mostly comedies. Or pro-grams where you have to guess how much the antiques are worth. Or people are buying houses or renovating and every-thing goes wrong until it's all fixed by the end of the show.

They smile, seem happy. *Really*, they are saying to her, *there's nothing to worry about except this. A system that works.* The rest is so incomprehensible it's a joke.

She watches the American President promising to fix something that he has ordered destroyed; she watches men in beards promising to destroy something they want fixed. Then they change places and words. She watches women in commercials who steadfastly psych themselves up to be improved, never looking beyond the edges of the screen.

She calls it realist-absurdism. But just to herself. She has always liked *isms*, always wanted one of her own. One of these days, she promises herself, she will tell the group.

Then there is the time before she took the medication.

It is a time of stark reality so brittle it takes all her energy to look. Everything is clear; all the denials are stripped away. There is no uncertainty.

The government and the corporations are out to screw us. Her husband has sold himself to his job and his entertainments. Her daughter makes herself impregnable and successful. Her friends feel sorry for her. Her family will tolerate her only if she plays within their script. Her intellectual insights are as irrelevant as the promises of that dream-only bridal night. Sex has deserted her, crawled up inside her body until the next rebirth.

Even then I dimly suspected enough to wonder where that's supposed to come from, she now thinks. *It's just another of His sick jokes.*

She takes refuge in warm spring days along the river. Birds, beaver, seals, fish, flies, flowers, trees. Dogs who have immediately forgotten the leash. The sun oozes over this world, reminds her of that strange memory: that a body could so effortlessly fill with fluid, rise up, turn towards such a sun, ready for any ecstasy.

MANNA

The dog sees it first. General Chang yaps a couple of mad challenges into the sky, then whines and runs so hard she yanks the line right out of my hand.

I look up. A body arrows straight for my head, arms flailing, dopplered scream rising as it plunges towards me. I freeze. Desperately want to move, but muscles lock in panic. Something bites me on the leg. I curse but the pain jolts me into leaping aside, and I fall down. The body explodes across the sidewalk beside me, and I'm drenched in blood. General Chang is suddenly there, lapping it up off my face.

Strange. Usually if she gets away from me she never comes back on her own. Maybe she really loves me.

The next thing I know I'm being interviewed by a young man with one blue and one green eye. He's in a police uniform, taking notes. Somebody has arranged me and the General on the nearest doorstep. The damn dog is now licking my splattered dress.

"Whose dog is that?"

"What?"

"The dog. Who does it belong to?"

"Me, of course. Is she a material witness?"

"Very funny. Just trying to figure out what happened here, ma'am."

"Seems obvious. Body falls from high-rise, hits sidewalk headfirst. Big splat. End of story."

"Do you know the bod—the deceased?"

"I don't even recognize what it was," I say, wearily. The shock is beginning to wear off, and I feel an odd disassociation, as if I could press a button and the whole thing would start over.

"You see anybody on the roof?"

"No. The only reason I jumped out of the way was because the dog went all hysterical and bit me."

"Why were you walking down this street?" He looks at me with those weird eyes. He's actually kind of cute, but I can't imagine letting those eyes look straight into me.

"I'm going home now," I say. "I'm very tired. You can phone me tomorrow, and we can discuss the weather further." I hate becoming involved in these things.

At this point a female cop comes over. She jerks her finger towards a squad car. "We've got a ride home for you," she says. "Looks like you could do with a cleanup."

I'm grateful and pick up General Chang. Behind me, I hear the young cop: "What kind of dog is that?"

"Shih Tzu," I say quietly. "She's a real killer."

Later, I'm stretched out luxuriously in a hot bath. General Chang is asleep on the edge of the bath mat. I am finally relaxed, thanks partly to a large Vermouth followed by my vibrator. It's the only way for me to get rid of real stress—my ex certainly wasn't up to it. I've got Boccherini on the CD player. Right after that it'll be Chantal Kreviazuk. I drift.

The dog sees it first. Her *yip yap yap* is like sharp fingernails playing my nervous system. I lurch into consciousness. The walls in my bathroom have become transparent. No, not just the bathroom, I see now: I can look right through the apartment wall. In fact, I can see out over the whole city. People are being pushed off rooftops. They must be screaming, but I can't hear them. Something terrible propels them. I get a glimpse of—something. Then the wall becomes solid again.

"Oh no," I say out loud to myself. "No, this is too much." A thought stops me—maybe I should be on medication. After all, isn't everyone?

Quickly, I get out of the tub, throw the towel around me, step on the stupid dog—"Sorry, sorry"—and rush over to the TV. For some reason I'm not panicked, just focused on wanting to know if this is coming from inside or outside my head. It seems very important.

The news channel isn't functioning. Well, it is sort of, but they've got one of those programs on where a clone couple is trying to choose between three separate homes.

The announcer, a slim oriental woman with black hair, strolls down a palm-lined street. She looks straight into the camera, right at me. "Darryl and Joan want a quiet place in the country near the beach," she says conversationally, "but close to shopping and city amenities, with enough space to add a pool should they decide to. Darryl wants a separate workshop as well, and Joan would like enough space for her two St. Bernards to be able to ramble safely outdoors. They're looking for a large front yard and don't want to be located on a busy street, yet they also would like nearby access to the freeway. In particular, they want a large older home that has all the amenities and is ready to move into, with at least seven bedrooms so there is enough space when all the family visit, and where everything has been updated. Finally, they're hoping to come in enough below budget that they can build a new three car garage on the property."

I change the channel. The same program is on. I flick through channel after channel. The friendly announcer sweeps her coloured hair back—but then I stop flicking and look more closely. Clearly this isn't the same announcer. For one thing, now she's not oriental. She's wearing an ugly necklace with fat beads, and—let's be honest—she's been into the ice cream at night big time. Her couple are called Lorenzo and Aristia. They're in northern Spain. Or is it Italy? Hard to tell, looking at the pine-covered hills.

On the next channel, a slightly different pair is in England with an anorexic blond who speaks with a posh accent she had to have learned in public school. "Of the three prop-ties we've shown Alex and Helen, which one will they choose? The more expensive estate with the horse paddock yet so close to the busy A24? Or the less expensive but brilliant townhome—with its large front garden—in the picturesque village of Little Squim? Or the updated condo only twenty minutes from London in the suburban village of Tittle-cum-cum? Let's find out." Cut to Alex and Helen looking coyly into the camera. After a prescient pause Helen says, "And we chose—."

But I don't give a damn. I turn to the next channel and the next and the next. They're all selling the relocation-vacation dream.

What's going on? What should I do now?

General Chang looks up at me, but she also is without strategy. Her gaze is the equivalent of a dog shrug. I throw down the channel changer and the TV dies in mid-sentence. Calmly, I sit and wait. Surely there is a revelation at hand.

Silence seems to have descended on the city outside my window although if I listen closely, I can hear the fluttering sound of beating paper wings, like a thousand silk moths faintly fanning the air. Are these the souls of the dead rising from their bloody pavement? Where will they go? Heaven doesn't seem like the right option here. More likely they are being harvested by the alien presence that has pushed them to their horrible death. I run this idea past General Chang, but she turns her head up at me in impatient puzzlement, demanding food.

"It's too bad the old *X-Files* isn't still on," I mutter, getting up to shred a cold chicken breast, "That Mulder would know what to do." On the way to the fridge, I look back as she patters behind me—and freeze. Are those flecks of fresh blood at the corners of her mouth? I was certain I had cleaned her off when we got home. Self-consciously, she licks her lips. Looks like guilt to me.

"What have you been up to?" I whisper as I slowly tear the cooked chicken breast into small pieces. She stares at me with maniacal concentration, as if I were God about to drop manna from the sky. Yet when I put the dish with the chicken bits down, she is not interested. Instead, she swivels her head towards the apartment door. I can't hear anything, but sure enough a few seconds later someone—or something—is pounding on it.

Now would be a great time to be able to look through the walls like I did before, but there is no way I can seem to make it happen. When I check out the peephole, all I see is what looks like blue sky, frothy white streamers floating across it. I back away, afraid to reach for the door handle.

The dog barks once, and the handle turns...and...with a little creak, the door slides open. I can't breathe.

"Hi."

It's Mrs. Krim from next door. Behind her is the cop from this morning. I remember the one blue and one green eye. He grins at me, but he's looking at my breasts. That freaks me out even more, and I pull my robe tighter.

Krim screws her mouth up in what she thinks is a smile, waving her hand. "Hiya, Beverly. Nice day isn't it?" She's a shrunken old gorgon whose pushed-in face, now that I come to think of it, makes her look quite a bit like my dog. She's always interrupting me at the weirdest times, wanting to talk about the weather. I wish General Chang would take a bite out of her, but for some reason the dog likes her. I think maybe Krim feeds her raw meat when I'm not looking.

"Huh?"

"Well, they said it was going to rain cats and dogs but hasn't so far. Say. This young man wants to ask you a few questions."

"What?"

"No, love. *He* wants to ask *you* the questions." She bends down to pat General Chang, who slurps on her fingers. "Now what have you been eating today, sweetie? Nothing that will upset your tummy I hope."

I am so stunned that I back into the room and they follow. The cop pulls out his notebook and starts writing. Krim offers him a seat, takes one herself, and says to me, "Well? What are you waiting for? Take a load off." I fall into a chair and the dog hops up on me. She still smells faintly of blood.

Krim points towards me. "She's a nice girl," she says to the cop. "Write that down."

He nods. "Okay," he says. "'*Nice.*' Got it. Now. If you don't mind, ma'am, I'd like to know a bit more about this dog of yours."

I can't contain myself any longer. "I want to know what's happening!" I wail. "Why are people being pushed off buildings? What about the ones on the street? Are they dying too? Why can I sometimes see through walls? *What's going on?*"

He looks at me, his weird eyes again hitting my breasts first, then moving upward. I shiver. "Haven't you been watching TV?" he asks. "They've been covering it all day."

"You think I'm an idiot? Of course I turned on the TV. But every channel had that program where people buy houses or vacation spots."

He shakes his head. "Huh," he says. "Well, that's a clue, isn't it. Now, about the dog, ma'am."

I stare at the cop. He's lost his cuteness, definitely. Out of the corner of my eye, a shadow plunges past the nearest window, arms flailing, a hollow cry trailing after.

"If I could have your attention, please," the cop says. "Like I said, I really need to get some particulars on that dog. You said it was a Shizoo. I've got that down already. But what about its personality? Does it have any special abilities? Like any—how can I say this—heightened sensory projection that would unduly influence you? Pull you out of the normal world, so to speak?"

His pen hovers over the notebook, waiting for my answer.

But I say nothing. I can't trust my brain anymore. I turn my head so I can see through the open door into what used to be the hallway beyond my apartment. There's a desert out there. Sand dunes stretch to the horizon, painfully luminous in the burning sun. The fear of an immense unknown overwhelms me. I look at General Chang. She looks up at me, licking her bloody lips.

I have no idea what will happen next. Terrified, I fix my gaze on her as if my life depends on it. Like a dog waiting for a piece of meat to fall to the floor.

IN THE INFINITE, THE MOMENT

About sixty kilometres north of Saskatoon, near Hague, she remembered one part of it.

Her first emotion was anger. "He made me," she said through clenched teeth. The transmission clunked into a lower gear as she shifted and slowed for the Shell station ahead. The old Chevy Suburban didn't feel quite right, but she hadn't driven it that much. It was/had been his.

"Sorry," she said to it, "I didn't mean to."

As soon as she stopped beside the pump, the attendant came out and when she didn't open the door, he tapped on the window. She lowered it several inches.

"What d'you want?" she said.

He looked at her, confused. "Um, want me to fill it up?" He was wearing a baseball cap that said "Air Bearings" on the front. She saw him sneak a quick look at her breasts. Well, that didn't mean anything.

"If that's what you want," she said.

While he was busy at the back of the vehicle, she got out and walked towards the office. Of course they wouldn't know yet. It would take them a while, so she decided to live for the moment. A moment could be a thousand universes. She'd heard that on a radio program about the Sufis, or maybe it was the Buddhists. Something to do with spaces and the energy within them. Apparently, living between the hard points of the ordinary world was a way to experience infinity.

Inside, she got the washroom key from a bored girl who was leafing desultorily through the *Saskatoon StarPhoenix*.

"That's a great name for a newspaper," she said to the girl as she took the key.

The girl looked up at her. "Huh?"

"It's kind of mythic."

"Huh?"

Inside the washroom, she carefully put toilet paper around the seat and then looked at it. *I don't have to pee*, she thought. Instead, she splashed cold water and then searing hot water over her face. Her hands were shaking. The lower part of her stomach felt funny. *Maybe I've got that virus. Or maybe it's my period.* Then she corrected herself. *No, I just finished my period last week.*

In front of the young woman once more, she asked, "Do you sell booze here? I need to drink while I drive."

"Huh?" the girl sat back, her mouthed screwed up.

"Nevermind," she said. "I'm joking. I'll take this Coke Zero.

Kurt Cobain wouldn't care." Before the girl could say *huh* again, she threw five twenty dollar bills on the counter and walked out. She passed the attendant on the way in. He looked at her breasts and said, "That's $64.53. I couldn't get it to $65."

"Okay," she waved and kept walking. "Keep the change."

The road sign said she was heading for Prince Albert and/or Waskesiu. "How far should I go?" she asked the Suburban. It changed gears now with a definite thunk. "You're not feeling well," she said. "I should have got you something at the gas station. No worries, we'll have a rest later."

She turned on the radio, hoping for something from the eighties, but the announcer immediately said in a voice attempting the dramatic, "Saskatoon police are investigating a probable missing person's case and would like the public's help. Apparently—"

She turned the radio off. *I'm not helping them with anything. I'm not the public.*

Golden November sunlight streamed through the rear windows of the Suburban. It drove smoothly now, and she watched large machines flatten clay and dirt along the side of the highway. By this time next year, it would be twinned all the way to Prince Albert. But that was an eternity. The weather was warm for early November, a couple degrees above freezing.

"El Niño sending me a message," she said and smiled.

Always look on the bright side, Meredith, her dead grandmother intoned. Jesus, how many years had she been saying that?

"Grampa bored you to death," she told her grandmother. "That's a crime in itself. Sixteen hours of cable television a day after he retired. I rest my case."

She was approaching P.A. There was a sign at a dirt road that wavered off into the bush. The sign said: "Children's Bible Camp."

For a moment, she hesitated. It might be the right thing to do. But then she thought of the prophet Elisha, who had come home after a hard day's work of trying to persuade the pig-headed Israelites to listen to God or else—but nobody was paying attention. As he trudged home in the hot dust, no cable television to look forward to, a bunch of young people ran after him, teasing him about his slovenly appearance and, especially, about his bald head. It was too much. And not fair after all he'd tried to do for everybody. And it was hot out. And he had a bad headache. God had said he could, so he called down divine wrath on those terrible youths. And behold, two female bears rushed out of the hills and tore all the kids to bloody mangled shreds. She imagined Elisha saying to himself, "They made me."

The Bible didn't say what he told their parents.

She drove on. It wasn't time to surrender.

In P.A., she got a room at the Super 8. It had satellite television and wireless Internet, but she didn't turn on the TV, and she'd left her computer in Saskatoon. Instead, she went out for a Chinese food smorgasbord. The restaurant was owned by First Nations people who were very polite.

As she paid the bill, the rather chunky but friendly older cashier asked, "How's everything, eh?"

"Everything was fine," she said, and made herself smile. Once outside the door, however, she added, "It just isn't fine anymore."

She came back to the motel and sat in the tub for a while, and then she remembered to turn on the taps.

In the morning she woke up to her wide open eyes staring at the ceiling. There were no pictures there, so she rose and was soon in a buffet joint called Friendly Franks that served pancakes, bacon, pickled eggs, and kielbasa Ukrainian sausage—"And Everything in Between"—the sign over the buffet table said.

A chemical blonde waitress in her early forties bubbled and frothed. "Well, isn't it just a lovely day! Y'know, we have a jail with razor wire down the street at the end of the block. Prince Albert has a lot of jails and a penitentiary. It's not a very nice city. Gangs. Drugs. Worse than Regina. Before, the, y'know, natives used to stay outside on their reserves, and we stayed here. Out of each other's hair, eh. But, like, now they've come in and want everything. Y'know, I'm not so sure we should give it to them. Tea or coffee, honey?"

Meredith looked straight at her. "I vant to be alone."

The waitress straightened up. "Oh." She quickly adjusted her program. "You have a real nice day." She turned and bounced off, humming to the background country & western muzak of Tim McGraw.

It wasn't until Meredith headed into the valley down Highway 2—downtown P.A. on her right in the dusty sunshine and the Diefenbaker Bridge over the North Saskatchewan in front of her—that she knew she was going to go farther north. A sign offered her Waskesiu and then La Ronge.

"We'll just have to see about that," she said.

The Suburban hauled her over the bridge and up out of the valley. Soon, flat fields and a wide sky stretched around her. Patches of naked poplars, birches, and tamaracks clumped in ever-thickening numbers as she travelled farther north. Eventually, even the hayfields were replaced by forest that became

123

dense with pine, spruce, and fir. It didn't look like they would be able to find anyone in this. But at the same time, her twenty-first century mind told her the satellites were *at this very second* taking notes in the hard particle radiation of space. Her one hope was in the essential inefficiencies of a culture that firmly believed itself to be operating in the rationalist tradition even as it lived a delusional belief in endless consumption. She put her faith in people who lied to themselves and who relied on machines that eventually broke down.

Thinking this through made her feel better.

It was remarkable, actually, how she couldn't remember much about him or what exactly had happened. Her first memory was that she had done something terrible, so she had to go on that.

A cop car abruptly wailed behind her, maniacal lights flashing back and forth. It raced up to tailgate her, and she felt her stomach drop and couldn't breathe. Her foot was frozen on the pedal. Fortunately, the Suburban held true and steady at the speed limit on the road. The cop stayed close behind, then burst around beside her, gave her a dirty look, and sped off up the highway. Soon the Mountie disappeared over a far hill.

She pulled over to the side of the road, somehow remembering to put her flashers on. She carefully turned the vehicle off and sat still, encouraging her body to breathe, her hands tight to the steering wheel. After a while the gulping stopped, and she discovered she'd peed her pants a little so she stuffed Kleenex down there and forgot about it. She recalled that the Suburban's speedometer was a little whacky, always showing faster than it really was. *Albert Einstein*, she thought. *I guess he was right. That's probably why that cop was so pissed. I was going too slow for his frame of reference.*

When she started the old Chev up, it lurched forward a few

feet and stopped dead. Her face burned. This was not good. She counted to twenty-five, then said a quick prayer. *I'm sorry for not taking Elisha seriously. Please don't let the bears eat me.* When she turned the key, the engine roared to life; when she put her foot on the pedal, the Suburban accelerated smoothly onto the highway.

"Thank you," she said and meant it. "And thanks to the Sufis and the Buddhists too."

The worst part was her future. She felt like she had to dump all of it.

At the next rest stop, she got out and poured bottled water on her hands and on her head. Then she let out one deep, painful howl, like a she-wolf abandoned by her pack. She stood for a while, clenching her fists, finally getting back in the Chev to continue on. What else was there to do? She knew it would all come back to haunt her. But right now she didn't want to think of one single person whose spirit was entangled with hers.

She whispered to herself, "The infinite, the moment" to the rhythm of the Suburban's tires on the pavement, "... the infinite, the moment."

For a long time, there was a blank, yellow sun and dark forest.

Eventually, she found herself parked at the side of the highway, another road veering off west to the left. Several metres on the road straight ahead a sign said "La Ronge 125." Once every fifteen minutes or so, a car would pass her, heading north.

"This is it," she told the Suburban. "The fork in the road."

Her brother offered some advice. *Turn left. Go to Waskesiu.* In a flood of memory, she abruptly knew he was now somewhere in the southern Sudan. Was it Darfur? He'd gone there on some Christian outfit called Youth With A Mission. But he'd always referred to it as YWAM.

"Don't go there," she'd told him. "It's a dangerous place."

"Jesus will protect me," he had answered her, that stupid, simple smile stuck on his face.

"Dammit, Vern, you're reacting on impulse to unconscious emotion from some problem you haven't dealt with. Don't trust that. Or those Y-WAMMers—what a dumb name." Then she'd made the mistake of adding, "Nobody believes in Christian crap anymore. Please don't go. I'm afraid."

A month later, he'd sent her an email with the details of one of his "adventures." They had been out in one of the villages, he said, escorted by government troops. This in itself was a problem because the rebels were occupying the village, and he said that when these rebels revealed themselves and came out with machetes and Kalashnikovs, the government troops took off "like spooked white-tailed deer." While the missionaries were standing there with flies crawling over them, the rebels waving their weapons, Vern had a sudden inspiration. "*You* know where it came from," he'd written, mysteriously. He had walked out towards the villagers. They told him later the leader of his missionary group was crying and pleading with him not to go because they'd all be killed. Meredith imagined him walking out to be met by a bearded man waving his machete and yelling, "I cut off your head, infidel!"

Some terrible force had taken over his body, Vern said. It thrust his arm forward so his finger was pointing at the angry man in front of him. It made him shout, "You need Jesus Christ! Your soul is going to hell! You need Christ! Now!"

According to Vern, a "miracle" then occurred. The man had

126

fallen to his knees as if he'd taken a blow to the gut. When he'd raised his head, Vern saw tears in his eyes, and the man had said, "What I have to do to get me save?" The Y-WAMMers then entered the village and an orgy of conversions lasted well into the night.

She put her head against the steering wheel. "What do I have to do, Suburban?" It didn't answer.

As she started up and took the turn to the left, she thought about Vern's story and the automatic weapons. That made her wonder. But there was no memory. Nothing. She thought she must have phoned her best friend, Vickie. Of course she would have phoned Vickie. With one hand, Meredith reached for her cellphone, but it wasn't in her purse. In fact, there wasn't much in her purse. Her new mini makeup kit wasn't even there. Most of the contents consisted of the big wad of bills she'd found in it as she drove out of Saskatoon.

The Suburban swerved on an ice patch, and she put both hands back on the wheel. "We don't want to have an accident," she said to it.

The Village of Waskesiu was virtually deserted, but she did see a sign for the RCMP station and there was a cop car in front of it—it looked like the one that had passed her—and at that point a cute, young uniformed guy came out of the door, resting his hand on the gun in his holster at his hip. Fortunately, he didn't look her way, and she quickly turned down a side street and drove past the park. There was a nice gazebo at the edge of Waskesiu Lake, beyond it the water a dark aquamarine under the angled sun.

She went down another street and then back out of the village, following the road west around the north side of the lake and away from the main road that went back to the highway. She passed no one. The sun warmed her through the window and light scattered gems over the water. A steady rhythm of waves rolled across the wide lake. It was peaceful. Empty. She imagined how gloomy it was beneath those dark green waves. She knew the water was beautiful but dangerous.

Where the pavement ended, a narrow gravel road went further west and north, but she didn't go there. It looked icy and forbidding beneath the perpetual shade of the tall, dark spruce lining the road. Instead, she pulled into a wilderness picnic area that fronted south on the lake and got out of the Suburban to walk along the shore. A breeze brought fresh oxygen off the water, tinged with something darkly organic. The waves were not transparent; they slopped bark and leaf sludge over the sand. Across the lake far to the south, she saw a line of hills.

"Why am I here?" she asked, tears not far away.

When she tried to start the Suburban, it died. She tried again; it coughed to life, but when she attempted to drive forward the transmission locked and it bucked and died again. This time it wouldn't start.

"Oh," she said. She looked for transmission fluid in the back, thinking that might be the problem, but there was nothing. He was terrible that way. She allowed herself an indulgent smile; he was always living for the moment, never planning for emergencies. Then she remembered something else.

"The infinite, the moment," she began to repeat quickly to herself.

It was warm in the Suburban until the sun set. As the dark crawled over her, so did the cold. Even through the Suburban's metal, she imagined she could feel the icy wind-fingers off the lake, yet that soon died into an implacable calm. Painfully bright stars filled the sky; there was no moon.

Shivering, she cried herself into the dark.

The next thing she saw was warm sun slanting through a window. She was in a bed, covered in blankets. In fact, she was hot. A wood stove filled the air around her with smoky heat.

"Are you all right?" a male voice said behind her. He moved around to where she could see him. He wasn't drop-dead cute, but he was slim and had good shoulders. Okay-attractive. "I found you in your Suburban," he continued. "Way back at the picnic site. At first I thought you were dead, but you're not. Obviously." He smiled in a kind of self-deprecating way: definitely non-threatening. "Anyway. I'm glad you're okay. You are okay, right?"

She made a quick inventory. "Yes," she nodded, "I'm fine."

"Good!" he said. "Let's eat."

Over the course of the next few days, he told her he had won the lottery. A very large amount. It had terrified him so much he'd decided to live in a log cabin with no gas, electricity, or running water. The cabin was situated far back in the bush at the edge of a small lake west of Prince Albert National Park.

She asked what the name of the lake was. (Really, where is it on the map, can the satellites see it).

He told her it was My Lake Waskesiu.

"But—" she said.

"Oh that's just what I call it. It probably has an official name in some computer in Regina or Ottawa, but I like this name." He smiled. "No relation to the big lake in the park."

He told her that when he wanted to get out for supplies, he followed an old logging road west to Highway 922 and then down to Big River. They even had a hospital there.

"Where's my Suburban!" she demanded, panic flashing through her.

He hooked a thumb towards the side of the cabin. "I fixed it and brought it up here." He looked at the ceiling. "You were out of it for quite a while. Not sick really, just . . . not here yet."

They lived together. When the road out became a bog in the spring and fall, they were marooned at the cabin for long periods of time. Intermittently, she asked him questions about his past. He answered her but told her nothing beyond the minimum.

Eventually it was clear that no one would come looking for her. Like the Suburban, My Lake Waskesiu became her friend. She took the trail her lover had bushwhacked out around the lake, sharing her partially returning memories with the water and the trees. Often she would talk to the big old Chev.

But there were still large blanks. Sometimes, when he did something that really irritated her, she looked at her hands, afraid she might do something. Apparently she had done it before.

One evening after they had made love and were drinking hot chocolate by the heat of the wood stove, he told her he was an "amateur Sufi," and he laughed. She thought that odd.

When it was clear at night, she watched the satellites; they moved rapidly across the night sky in the spaces between the stars. She sometimes waved—and then panicked, cringing away under the trees.

She said to herself, *Meredith, one day you'll have to go outside and face the consequences. You'll have to see those people again. You'll have to find out what you did.*

But for a long time everything stayed the same in the infinite, the moment, and she was happy.

THE PAINTED HAND

The red painted hand represents courage and honour. To demonstrate their superiority, young warriors would charge their horses into the enemy, touching and imprinting their painted hands on their foe or the flanks of their war ponies. It is a form of counting coup.

I wake up in Mr. Jimmy's BMW. We're parked in front of the casino, but the rest of the lot is empty. The painted hand sign looms over me like a stop sign. *Too late*, it says to my head.

I hear him laughing quietly behind me, his voice thick with smoker's death. I know he does that to intimidate me.

"Guess I lost it all, eh." I sigh. My head hurts.

We always win a little... he growls.

"...but lose everything in the end." I finish for him. "I know it by heart now. Your version of optimism."

I never promised you a rose garden, accompanied by a snicker.

"Okay, okay. I heard enough of that song last night." I turn quickly, trying to get a glimpse of him. But he's too fast for me. So I slump back down in the front seat and grab the steering wheel for support.

I just need something. A little luck. I'm the kind who picks the wrong lineup in the supermarket. My turn comes up and the lady in front of me, the kid in front of me, the fat man in front of me drops her/his coins on the floor, wants another bag of candy, says he forgot his wallet can you put it on my credit, you don't have any credit, okay can you ask the manager, fine says the cashier, but you'll have to wait a minute, sorry folks I'll try to be right back, but she isn't.

I'm also the kind of woman who wants the look of danger in a guy's eyes but not the substance: he knows the thoughts but never acts on them. Well. Except occasionally in bed when I want him to.

"Gotta pee," I say.

When you're finished being biological, I've got another adventure for you.

I hate it when Mr. Jimmy speaks and you can't see him. Which is most of the time.

After grabbing some Kleenex, I get out of the car and try to hide myself between the west side of the casino and the next building. Thank god Yorkton, Saskatchewan is dead this time of the morning. But come 8:00 or 9:00, whenever the honey-pot opens up, they'll start circling it, some pretending to look at the *Counting Coup* statue out front before the orgasmic hope sucks them in again to lose what little is left.

"Won't be me, I don't have anything to gamble wi—"

Don't know about that, he says. *Think I might have a solution.* He's standing in front of me.

"Jesus!" I try to jump up out of a peeing squat and dribble on my panties.

Here. He hands me some more Kleenex. *I always liked girls better*, he says, turning and wandering towards the car.

"Wait, you bastard!" I yell. "What d'you mean by 'solution'?"

I can clearly see this version of him: skinny, mid-40s, a little goatee, lank hair; looks like a failed RCMP biker informer.

He turns to me, walking backwards, shaking his head. Waves a finger—and everything changes.

My grandmother's kitchen is just the way I left it the last time I was here.

That in itself stops me: is my experience just a copied file that's rewritten slightly every visit? I look at her more closely. Maybe her red hair is streaked whiter, and is a little more ragged than the previous time.

"You bring him with you?" She's bent over, brushing her chaotic hair with long, vigorous strokes. It's like mare's tail clouds flailing across a windswept sky. I can't see her face, but I think she's laughing because her ample bosoms are jiggling. That's what she calls them: "bosoms."

"He's never far away, granny. You know that."

She grunts and surges upwards, a force, throws her head and hair back, looks me in the eye. "He hangs around like a dirty shirt. I know you won't listen to me about the men you handle, but I've always told you trust is everything in a man. The ones with that look of danger. They're just for a wild ride now and then. Never keep 'em around."

I'm shocked. She has never talked like this with me before. Usually, she's all about marriage forever and you've got to do anything to hold onto them, live with whatever shit they throw at you because a woman alone is going nowhere. Maybe what I said the last time I was here hit home. I told her to take a good look at grandpa and where sticking with him has got her.

Then and now she looks around the shack they live in. A converted grain storage shed that grandpa split into a two story. Rat infested, no running water. On the way to the outside, you pass through a back- covered entranceway filled with old bicycle junk, car parts, stacks of old newspapers. Yeah, the rats love it. Then there's the winter when the woodstove gets so hot you can imagine grandpa's cigarette as a starter falling from his drunken fingers and the wood stove taking over. In one minute the whole dry-stick mess up in flames.

"Yes I've changed my mind," she says, explaining nothing. "I know me and I know you. You're a gambler. Always trying to believe the next hand will be a rescue. You can leave things to chance up to a point, but once you make up your mind, don't take chances. Control. That's what you need, little wild thing. Control your men and control your life."

I remember that grandpa is dead. Or is that in a later scenario? Anyway, he's not here now. She does seem way more assertive and independent. So I'm getting a little afraid for her. Mr. Jimmy doesn't like this kind of thing. Is that his hacking laughter I can hear whispering from the junk in the back entrance?

"I'm fine," I say. "He's fine. Everything's okay, granny."

She shakes her head and sighs, "No it isn't. Not yet, anyway. But you can't put an old head on young shoulders. I'm for bed." She rises slowly, groaning. "Oh my aching bones. I swear after one more day of work at that hospital they're going to have to carry me out with the slop. I'm getting old."

As she gives me a kiss, she whispers as she hugs me, "Wild one. Here's my love for you," breathing on me.

There are tears in my eyes as I watch her labour up the shack's creaking stairs to the bedroom. Is grandpa up there ready to start snoring the moment she gets into bed? Or is he out in the night, beating up people after a hard night in the bar? Or is he gone somewhere else? Maybe he's chasing my mother in hell. She likes to imagine that.

Well that was a nice interlude, Mr. Jimmy says, his voice is getting higher, more feminine. Which is not good.

I'm still in the car, still with a pounding headache. I search around in my purse that has everything in it but what I want. Finally find two extra-strength Tylenols and make myself swallow them. Ugh.

It's only then I realize we're also still in front of the casino. Wait. No, it's not the same one. This is *The Northern Lights*. How the——? But I know this place. Prince Albert, Saskatchewan. A good four hundred kilometres northwest of Yorkton.

Damn. He's done it again.

I'm runnin' you tonight, he says. *And you're gonna love it.*

Although I am about to whine, I know it's true. I can feel the surge of adrenalin, the throbbing between my legs. What granny doesn't understand is that I have no choice. I'm addicted to it, to him. It's just too damn exciting. Or does she know this? Is this what happened to her with grandpa?

It's the perverseness of human beings——the governed or the governing——that is my pleasure, Mr. Jimmy says matter-of-factly. *That's what I'm addicted to. Now get your fat ass in there and get me some stimulation.*

"My ass isn't fat," I say in my best little girl voice.

Mr. Jimmy sighs. *You're right. It's not. Forgive the gratuitous abuse.*

"I don't have any money."

Well...get some, whore! It's not like you haven't done it before.

As I push myself out of the car, trying to straighten up my clothes and hair, I see a couple of young businessmen hanging around just outside the entrance as the native and white poor of Prince Albert surge through the door, which makes a sucking sound each time it opens and closes.

I sidle up to the power-hungry guys, give them my best line, and soon they're following me as I waltz my not-fat ass for them. Once we're into their waiting limo where it's warm, I say, "What'll it be. I'll do anything if the price is right."

They both grin. The chunky one nudges the cute one with the beginnings of a man in him, who then says with theatrical aggression, "Proofread three contracts and check a fracking assessment." Then he remembers to add, "Bitch. We'll watch."

I should have known: Calgary oilmen. They're still everywhere these days, lubricating, fucking, and sucking Canada dry.

I cringe—talk about being a whore—but I think of the reward and gulp, nodding. "Okay. Pull them out. Let's see what your hard drives have got."

When I'm done, I take a shot of whisky from one and get out of the car. My legs are shaky, and my stomach doesn't feel so good. Electronic overload. God, I hate whoring, but that's the only way to get money these days.

Good girl, Mr. Jimmy whispers in my ear as I head for the casino entrance.

The first thing you notice once you're inside are the two ATM cash machines, followed by an intimidating bouncer to your right. On your left there's a counter with a multitude of clerks waiting to explain to you how to lose. Far to the right, and partially hidden behind all the slots, is another counter with eight windows where you can cash in your winnings. Only one window is open. And the guy lounging in front of it is talking to his friend inside.

That's all you need to know about casinos.

The place is packed—I think it's Friday night. No one is laughing; no one is smiling except the staff manning the tables, and then only if someone is playing their game.

I notice a curious fact: the only healthy looking people in this building are those working here. All First Nations. Same was true at *The Painted Hand*. The Saskatchewan Indian Gaming Commission runs these places. I make eyes at one tall, broad-shouldered guy in his thirties with sleek, black hair and a pony tail. He sure looks doable.

Remember why you're here! hisses Mr. Jimmy. *You get what I want, and I might throw a piece of the action your way after.*

"Okay," I mutter.

The dealer at the poker table eyes me strangely, like I'm weird. Or crazy.

I walk over to the nearest security, a big native woman projecting stern no-nonsense implacability. With eyes downcast, I show her the cash. She's momentarily startled, but quickly recovers, now understanding. She leans forward. I get a perverse thrill: I suddenly know she's gay.

"Okay," she says in a rich contralto voice. "I'll watch."

I give her my very best little girl. Being with Mr. Jimmy helps a lot there.

Slowly, very slowly, her eyes on me like a hawk, I begin: down on my hands and knees, laying the money bill by bill over the floor around her. Occasionally I look up. Her whole body trembles, her eyes are half-closed; she's breathing in short intake gasps.

It seems a long time that I am on the knife edge of exquisite humiliation. And yet also power because of the effect I'm having on her. Part of me never wants to let this go. Another part wants to kick me in the ass.

Eventually, all the money is down. Security sighs. She gives me the briefest of smiles and says, "That was good. Now get lost."

It's like being yanked away from total immersion. I stumble out of the casino.

It's winter now and unbelievably cold. A couple of guys are lying beside some cars, frozen no doubt, waiting to be picked up by the freezer unit in the morning.

Mr. Jimmy is strangely quiet when I get back in the car. After a while he says, almost hesitantly, *You didn't want that guy?*

"No. I lost my appetite."

So you want an intermission.

I nod, so weary I can hardly hold my head up. "Yeah. I need a rest."

He shrugs, *Okay. Until next time. Remember, I'm never far away.*

The cabin smells of the pitch-filled pine crackling in the wood stove. Outside the wind is soughing through tamarack, spruce, and poplar. In the small window, she can see a full moon rising above the lake, a silver island beneath it.

Her cell and iPad are turned off and out of sight. There is peace.

For now this is a haven, almost a heaven.

But not quite. Money sits on the table, waiting for the eventual arrival, even in this sacred space, of what will have to be done for its owners. She avoids looking there, instead stands and moves to the mirror hanging beside the window. In it, she sees the faint, coloured imprint of a hand on her cheek.

ABOUT THE AUTHOR

Alban Goulden was born in Yorkton, Saskatchewan. He later attended Lethbridge Junior College, the University of Alberta, and Simon Fraser University. He has published one previous book of short stories, *In the Wilderness* and two sci-fi novels, *HOME 1: Departure* and *HOME 2: Journey*. Goulden has published stories, essays, and poems in *Iron, Grain*, and *subTerrain*, and taught English Literature for many years at Simon Fraser University and Langara College. Goulden divides his time between Empress, Alberta and his home in New Westminster, BC. He is currently working on a new collection of stories, *Travels with Mr. Jimmy.*